普通高等教育"十一五"国家级规划教材

大学英语自主系列教材

总主编　余建中

主　编　季佩英　黄

编　者　景　蓉　俞蓓迪

U0132753

College English Listening

大学英语听力

自主

Guidance Book

指南

4

高等教育出版社

Higher Education Press

图书在版编目(CIP)数据

大学英语自主听力指南 . 4/余建中总主编;季佩英,黄莺分册
主编 . —北京:高等教育出版社,2009.5
ISBN 978 - 7 - 04 - 026539 - 2

Ⅰ. 大… Ⅱ. ①余…②季…③黄… Ⅲ. 英语 - 听说教学 -
高等学校 - 教学参考资料 Ⅳ. H319.9

中国版本图书馆 CIP 数据核字(2009)第 065231 号

策划编辑	陈锡镖	叶春阳	**责任编辑**	王雪婷	**封面设计**	王 峥
责任印制	陈伟光					

出版发行	高等教育出版社	购书热线	010 - 58581118
社 址	北京市西城区德外大街 4 号	免费咨询	800 - 810 - 0598
邮政编码	100120	网 址	http://www.hep.edu.cn
总 机	010 - 58581000		http://www.hep.com.cn
		网上订购	http://www.landraco.com
经 销	蓝色畅想图书发行有限公司		http://www.landraco.com.cn
印 刷	北京市白帆印务有限公司	畅想教育	http://www.widedu.com
开 本	889×1194 1/16	版 次	2009 年 5 月第 1 版
印 张	12	印 次	2009 年 6 月第 2 次印刷
字 数	380 000	定 价	20.00 元

物料号 26539 - 00

前　言

随着我国改革开放日益深化及加入世界贸易组织,社会各领域参与国际交流的机会越来越多,新的社会需求对大学生的英语能力提出了更高的要求,教育部制定的《大学英语课程教学要求》也提出了新的大学英语课程教学目标,即在培养学生英语综合运用能力的同时,增加其自主学习能力,提高综合文化素养,以适应我国社会发展和国际交流的需要。

鉴于现有的教学内容和教学学时不足以满足人才培养的需要,要切实保证大学英语课程教学目标的实现,我们需要充分利用学生的课余时间,激发学生课后的自主学习兴趣,提高他们的自主学习能力,不断扩大学生广泛接触英语的天地,使得他们的课堂学习内容在课后能得到进一步延伸。课后广泛的听说训练,不仅能使学生巩固课堂掌握的学习方法和学习策略,更能增加人文和科学知识,提高综合素养。

本套教材为现有大学英语教材的补充和延伸,与现有课堂教学内容交相辉映。我们期待本教材能够引导学生最终成为快乐的英语学习者、终身的英语学习者、集技能与策略于一身的英语学习者,从而使《教学要求》的目标最终得以实现。

本套教材的编者充分研究了国内外各种英语听力教材的编写特点,从思想性、知识性、科学性、人文性、时代性、实用性及趣味性等多角度入手,以注重打好语言基础为出发点,同时注重培养学生的实际应用能力。

本套教材的特点是:

1. 强调自主学习特征。作为对现有大学英语教材的延伸和补充,本套教材强调发挥学生在学习过程中的自主作用,每单元都以学习任务为出发点,反复操练,逐步深入,旨在有步骤、有目的地引导学生开发各种学习潜能。

2. 突出语料的真实性和语境的实用性。大量语料选自英、美人的日常生活会话,真实自然,便于学生今后对外交流时直接应用。

3. 注重文化信息。在注重英语语言基础知识和基本技能训练的同时,注意将文化内容与语言材料相融合,话题覆盖英美文化生活的方方面面。

4. 融教学与考查为一体。除了课文训练之外,本教材还有期中、期末自测题,供学生自我检查学习效果。

5. 辅助课堂教学。本套教材既可以用于学生自主学习,又可以作为普通听力教程。本教材配套指南包含了详细的学习目标与学习计划,对文化信息、语言信息也有相应的补充和解释。

6. 帮助学生应对大学英语四、六级考试。随着大学英语教学改革的深入,英语听力在大学英语教学和考试中的比重已经显著增加。本教材第三册的难度约与大学英语四级考试相当,第四册的难度在四级以上。因此,学完本教材的学生在听力方面不仅能够从容应对大学英语四级考试,还能挑战大学英语六级考试。

《大学英语自主听力》由复旦大学余建中教授担任总主编,本册主编是季佩英、黄莺,参加编撰的还有景蓉、俞蓓迪。

本教材是适应教育部《大学英语课程教学要求》全新理念的尝试和探索,由于编者水平所限,敬请广大师生在使用过程中多提宝贵意见和建议。

编者
2009 年 4 月

使 用 说 明

本套教材共分4册,每册共16个单元,并配有两套水平自测题。每单元按照不同的学习任务展开,题材广泛,涉及生活的各个领域。本册的各个单元由以下5个部分组成:

Part A   Language Focus

该部分是本单元的准备阶段,提供本单元基本词汇和部分句型。为方便学习者使用,句子或词组中较难的词汇用斜体表示,并加以中文注释。教师(如果上课使用本教材,以下省略)可以带领学生将所有词汇和句型通读一遍,并进行必要的解释和指导,使学生熟悉本单元的语境,预先融入到本单元的任务话题之中,为接下来的进一步语言训练做好准备。

Part B   Authentic Conversations

该部分基本由6段短会话、2段长对话组成,语料具有真实性和实用性,能够帮助学习者在真实语言情景中锻炼英语听力。

教师可以在操练前启发学生进入到会话情景中,让学生预先将注意力集中于相关语境。整个操练过程中,教师可以将重点放在指导学生有效获取听力信息,抓住交谈要点。如果时间和条件许可,可以根据实际情况适当增加模拟会话练习,反复操练基本听力任务。

Part C   Talks from Radio/TV Programs

该部分取材于英语国家的电台或电视节目,有人物介绍、新闻、故事、评论、访谈等内容,主要培养学生听懂英语电台广播、看懂英语电视节目的能力。

教师可以从大众传媒对公众影响的角度讲解这部分的练习,指导学生领会特定的语言表达。

Part D   Dictation

该部分主要训练学生的听写能力。学生在完成听写任务前,可以先熟悉一下有关生词或词组,以免在听写过程中无法继续。

Part E   Fun Time

该部分一般包含幽默故事、诗歌、英语成语、英语歌曲等,是轻松的英语娱乐时间,其目的是培养学生对英语语言学习的兴趣,并缓解听力训练给他们带来的紧张情绪。教师可以在学生听后组织各种活动,如对幽默故事的诙谐之处加以点评,朗诵诗歌、演唱英语歌曲等。课堂时间不足时,也可以由学生自行完成。

本册中所含的水平自测题完全按照大学英语四级考试的框架编写,但是内容跟试卷前面的各单元相关。

本《指南》包含教学目的、教学安排、听力文本、答案、注解等内容,学习者可以选择使用。

本套教材拟定两个学年完成,建议一学期完成一册的学习任务,每周安排一个单元。

编 者
2009 年 4 月

Contents

Unit 8　Aging

Test Yourself（Units 1～8）

Unit 9　Growing Pains

Unit 10　Technology

Unit 11　Newspapers

Unit 12　Helping Others

Unit 13　Social Customs

Unit 14　Making Complaints

Unit 15　Emergency

Unit 16　Talking About the Future

Test Yourself（Units 9～16）

Unit 1

Studying Abroad

Preview

This unit integrates various useful expressions and authentic talks about studying abroad.

Objectives

After studying this unit, the learners are expected to:
1. know the basic words and expressions about studying abroad;
2. understand conversations and short talks about life and studying abroad;
3. be able to seek information about studying abroad using the words and expressions learnt in this unit.

Part A Language Focus

Notes

1. subject, field, major

   Subject is an area of knowledge that you study at a school or university.

   e.g. *English is my favorite subject.*

   Field is a particular subject or activity that somebody works in or is interested in.

   e.g. *Professor Smith is one of the main experts in the field of animal behavior research.*

   Major refers to the main subject that a student studies at college or university.

   e.g. *a math major, an English major*

2. professor, associate professor, etc.

Academic rank varies in different countries. The commonest ranks in the United Kingdom are:

Professor

Reader

Senior Lecturer

Lecturer

The commonest ranks in the United States are:

Professor

Associate Professor

Assistant Professor

Instructor (sometimes "Lecturer")

Sometimes a full professor is awarded a specific, endowed chair named either after a founder or donor or in order to commemorate someone.

e.g. *the William Henry Bishop Professor* at Yale, *the Charles Eliot Norton Professor of Poetry* at Harvard

Generally, a named chair is more prestigious than one without a name.

Part B Authentic Conversations

Purpose

This part aims to familiarize the students with authentic conversations that can be heard in our daily life about studying abroad.

Detailed Plan

1. Study the new words and expressions in *Word Bank*.
2. Do the required exercises.
3. Check the answers.
4. Listen to the conversations again. Pay special attention to the parts you didn't understand or misunderstood. You may refer to the script if necessary.

Short Conversations

Listening Script

Directions: You will hear 6 conversations between two speakers. Listen to them and answer the following questions by choosing the right options.

1. Woman: Mr. Abebe, would you tell us something about yourself and how you came to the United States?

   Man: Well, my name is Daniel Abebe. I came from Addis Ababa, the capital city of Ethiopia. I came to the United States as an international student when I was 20, and it wasn't until I approached my 40th birthday that I became a citizen of the United States.

   Question: Which of the following description of Mr. Abebe is correct?

2. Woman: What language course did you take in high school?

   Man: I am interested in Chinese but I actually took French. I took French since Grade Three and then just kind of jumped at a scholarship that I'm getting next year. I'm studying abroad for the whole year, so I thought having some Arabic in an Arabic-speaking country would give me some help there.

   Question: What language is the man learning now?

3. Woman: Hi, Josh, what about the study abroad program for the anthropology students you joined?

   Man: Oh, well, it took me to China. I learned a little bit of the language there, taught in a small school, and made a lot of friends. Sometimes I felt like being a pop star.

   Question: What can we learn about Josh?

4. Man: Good afternoon. I'm an international student from Egypt, and I've been here for — I don't know, six years probably. I've just graduated from the student program here at the medical university.

   Woman: Yes. And you will be planning to head home soon?

   Man: Yes, actually I'm leaving in four days. I just talked to my advisor in New York to say goodbye.

   Question: Which of the following is not true about the man?

5. Woman: How can you receive so many scholarships? Eight altogether!

   Man: It's not just good grades. There are more average students that can also qualify for some scholarships as well. They are often based on an interest you have and your background. But get the information about colleges and their scholarships and start early. That's the No. 1 thing.

   Question: What does the man think is the most important for getting scholarships?

6. Man: There's a lot to go through with some of your students before they go traveling abroad. Are there some concerns you have about not allowing them to study in certain places?

   Woman: Absolutely, we make sure that information about safety and security is available to the students and their families. All of our students who study abroad have to acknowledge the risk inherent in travel and study abroad.

   Question: According to the woman, what must the teachers make sure before the students go traveling abroad?

Key

1. D 2. B 3. D 4. C 5. D 6. B

Notes

> **1. Addis Ababa**
>
> Addis Ababa is the capital of Ethiopia. It is also the largest city and commercial center of Ethiopia. The city is situated on a plateau in the central mountains of Ethiopia.
>
> **2. Ethiopia**
>
> Ethiopia is one of the largest and most populous countries in Africa. It is also one of the oldest countries in the world. It is located in northeastern Africa, in an area known as the Horn of Africa.
>
> With a population around 74,778,000, the average life expectancy at birth is about 45 years for males and 49 years for females.
>
> **3. an Arabic-speaking country**
>
> An Arabic-speaking country is one whose official language is Arabic. The Arabic language is one of the world's most widely used languages. It is the official language of many Arab nations in the Middle East and northern Africa, including Egypt, Iraq, Jordan, Lebanon, Saudi Arabia, and Syria.
>
> **4. Egypt**
>
> Egypt is a Middle Eastern country located in the northeast corner of Africa. The Nile River flows northward through the desert and serves as a vital source of life for most Egyptians. Most Egyptians consider themselves Arabs. About 90 percent are Muslims. Islam, the Muslim religion, influences family life, social relationships, business activities, and government affairs.

Longer Conversations

Conversation One

Listening Script

Directions: You will hear a conversation between two speakers. Listen to the conversation twice and answer the questions by choosing the right options.

Woman: What have you learned in your time here? Obviously, you've learned a great deal.

Man: Oh yes! See, I'm a Muslim. My advisor was Jewish. My, you know, co-workers were Catholic, Indians, Chinese — so the number one thing I learned from this six-year experience is you can be different from people, and yet, you still can be a friend. And you can interact with them easily. That's — I think the number one lesson even before — number two is lung cancer prevention, which is my field.

Woman：Two quick questions. What are you going to look forward to most when you get back home to Saudi Arabia?

Man：First，I'm really very excited that I will serve my country, serve Arabia in the field I got training education. Secondly，I'll be telling people that you have different kinds of people that you may interact with. They may think in a different way，than how you think. Yet，you can again live with them in a very peaceful way. I think that is a very important thing，I believe.

Woman：Yes，and I think that answered my second question. That was if the goal was mutual understanding. It sounds like it worked.

Questions：

1. What is the religious background of the man's advisor?
2. What is the most important lesson the man learned from his six-year experience?
3. What is the man so excited about?
4. What is the woman's second question concerned about?

Key

1. B   2. D   3. B   4. D

Notes

1. **Muslim**

    A Muslim is a follower or believer in Islam，who worships Allah（one and only God of Islam）alone and holds Muhammad（about 570—632）to be the last and chief prophet. Today，there are about 935 million Muslims worldwide.

    The word *Muslim* can also be used as an adjective.

2. **Jewish**

    Any person whose religion is *Judaism*（犹太教）is Jewish. In a wider sense，any member of a worldwide ethnic and cultural group descended from the ancient Hebrews is Jewish. Judaism has more than 14 million followers throughout the world. More than a third of those live in the United States. Many other Jews live in *Israel*（以色列）.

3. **Catholic**

    Any member of a Catholic Church, especially *Roman Catholic Church*（天主教会），is Catholic. Roman Catholic Church is the largest body of Christians in the world. It has about 1 billion members，nearly a fifth of the world's population.

4. **six-year experience**

    This refers to the six years through which the speaker completed his medical study in the USA.

5. **Saudi Arabia**

    Saudi Arabia is a large Middle Eastern nation that ranks as the world's leading producer of petroleum. Nearly all the people who live in Saudi Arabia are Arab Muslims.

6. **Arabia**

    Arabia refers to the *peninsula*（半岛）of Southwest Asia，bordering the Persian Gulf，the Arabian Sea，and the Red Sea. It includes the nations of Saudi Arabia，Yemen，Oman，the United Arab Emirates，Qatar，Kuwait，and the State of Bahrain.

Conversation Two

Listening Script

Directions: You will hear a conversation between two speakers. Listen to the conversation twice and answer the questions by choosing the right options.

Woman:	You actually got a full-ride to Stanford, is that right?
Man:	Yes, full tuition, room and board.
Woman:	OK, but you also got these additional scholarships. And just so people understand, the additional scholarships you got were very helpful to you throughout your college career, right?
Man:	Definitely. They helped pay for all my books, which are very expensive, and also my computer which is a large expense. Transportation back to my home city of Moscow. And a couple of extra fees that came up and things like that. But study abroad ... my scholarships did not cover all the expense.
Woman:	All right, so tell us how the search began for the scholarships.
Man:	Well, I started my junior year of high school investigating colleges that had a good business school, which is my major, and then also had good scholarships. Because I figured, one, I could get a big scholarship from a school which would cover everything. And if that didn't work out I'd get a whole bunch of little scholarships to cover it. And luckily both plans ended up working out for me.
Woman:	That's great! You did it.

Questions:

1. How did the additional scholarships help the student from Moscow throughout his college career?
2. What is the first important thing for the student to consider in selecting a college?
3. Why was the student able to get so many scholarships?

Key

1. D   2. B   3. C

Notes

1. Stanford

Stanford University, founded in 1885 by Senator Leland Stanford and his wife, is a leading educational and research center in the United States. It offers undergraduate and graduate courses of study, and about 25 of its graduate programs rank among the top 10 nationally in their fields. Stanford has schools of business, earth sciences, education, engineering, humanities and sciences, law, and medicine. These schools are divided into about 70 academic departments. In addition, Stanford is recognized as one of the world's leading centers of research in electronics and physics.

2. Moscow

Moscow is the capital of Russia and one of the largest cities in the world. More than 83 million people live in Moscow.

Part C Talks from Radio/TV Programs

Purpose

This part consists of exercises based on talks excerpted from radio/TV programs. The students are expected to understand such talks and get the necessary information from them.

Detailed Plan

1. Study the new words and expressions in *Word Bank*.
2. Do the exercises based on *Excerpt One* and *Excerpt Two*.
3. Check the answers.
4. Listen to the short talks again. Pay special attention to the parts you didn't understand or misunderstood. You may refer to the script if necessary.

Excerpt One

Listening Script

Directions: You will hear a short talk from a radio program. Listen to it twice and complete the following summary by filling in the blanks.

This is Talk of the Nation. I'm Neal Conan in Washington.

Since 9/11, more and more American students have been studying abroad. The number increased by almost 20 percent between 2001 and 2003. American students have become particularly interested in the non-English-speaking world. They're going to China, to India, and to the Middle East.

Living abroad can be a life-changing experience. It's a chance for an inside peek at another culture, to find new friends, learn different social rules, to see their country, your country and yourself through new eyes. People-to-people exchanges also help to humanize America and Americans in parts of the world where US policy may not be too popular.

For 60 years now, the Fulbright Program has sent US students abroad and brought foreign students to study in the US. The goal is mutual understanding. Recently, a group of students and scholars returned from Africa where they were working on a variety of projects. Today, we'll speak with a few of them about what it was like, what they learned, and how it's changed the way they look at the world.

Key

The number of American students studying abroad increased by almost 1) <u>20 percent</u> between 2001 and 2003. They have become particularly interested in the 2) <u>non-English-speaking</u> world. Living abroad can be a(n) 3) <u>life-changing</u> experience. It's a chance for 4) <u>an inside peek</u> at another culture, to see things and people through 5) <u>new eyes</u>. People-to-people exchanges also help to humanize America and Americans in places where US policy may not be 6) <u>too popular</u>. The goal is 7) <u>mutual understanding</u>. Today we will speak with some students and scholars who have returned from Africa.

Notes

1. **9/11**

   9/11 refers to the date of the massive terrorist attacks on the United States, resulting in the collapse of the World Trade Center's twin towers and surrounding buildings, and part of the Pentagon building. The attack occurred on September 11, 2001.

2. **Fullbright Program**

   The Fulbright Program is a program of grants for international educational exchange for scholars, educators, graduate students and professionals. The program was *conceived* (构想) by Sen. J. William Fulbright of Arkansas. It started in 1946 for students with B.A. or equivalent. In 1961, it was expanded to offer opportunities to teachers and researchers as well.

Excerpt Two

Listening Script

Directions: You will hear a short talk from a TV program. Listen to it twice and answer the questions by choosing the right options.

Graduating from any college or university in the United States is never an easy feat. For international students, that task is multiplied.

Today, Austin College graduated the class of 2008, and said good-bye to a student who has made his way around the world to complete a dream and help those back at home.

On a bright sunny day on the Austin College campus, thousands of hours of studying and hard work came to an end. As the cliché goes, graduation brings about the start of a new life; especially for Axel Nze Akoue.

After graduating high school, Axel received a scholarship from his native land to study in the United States. After spending a month in Chicago, trying to master the English language, he headed where a lot of students from Gabon go to study and continue their English studies: Grayson County College.

The transition from a place he had grown to love, to new surroundings, wasn't easy, but he fought through it, earning a degree in international studies and a minor in communication. Axel says he will now use those skills at the United Nations, working with the "Nothing but Nets" campaign to help combat malaria in African countries and it's that opportunity to give back which makes him special.

At the graduation ceremony, Axel and his senior classmates presented the college with a check for $51,000. All of the money will go to a scholarship for international students.

Questions:

1. Who faces the greatest difficulty while studying in a US college or university?
2. What is taking place on the Austin College campus?
3. Which of the following schools or colleges did Axel not attend before he began his study at Austin College?
4. What is Axel concerned about now that he has graduated from college?
5. Why do Axel and his classmates present the university with a check for $51,000?

Key

1. D 2. D 3. B 4. A 5. C

Notes

1. **Austin College**

   This is a private, coeducational institution of higher education in Sherman, Texas, US The college offers bachelor's degree programs in humanities, math and science, and social sciences, as well as interdisciplinary and area studies programs. A master's degree in education is also available.

2. **Gabon**

   Gabon is a country in west central Africa on the Atlantic coast. It became independent from France in 1960.

3. **Grayson County College**

   Grayson County College is a community college located in Grayson County, Texas. Grayson County is a county located in the US state of Texas. In 2007, the US Census Bureau estimated that its total population was 118,675.

4. **"Nothing but Nets" campaign**

   "Nothing But Nets" is a campaign to save lives by preventing malaria. Supported by the United Nations Foundation, it aims to stop the spread of malaria in African countries through the distribution and use of mosquito bed nets.

Part D Dictation

Purpose

This part contains a short talk to be dictated to the students. This exercise trains the students' skills in

writing down what they have heard.

Detailed Plan

1. Study the new words and expressions in *Word Bank*.
2. Listen to the short talk from the beginning to the end without any pause.
3. Write down the sentences during the pauses when the short talk is spoken again.
4. Read the listening script and correct whatever mistakes the students may have made.
5. Listen to the short talk again if necessary.

Listening Script

Directions: You will hear a short talk encouraging more students to pursue higher education abroad. The short talk will be spoken twice. After you listen to it at normal speed, the short talk will be spoken again with pauses. During the pauses, write down what you hear in the space provided below.

There is no question in my mind that pursuing higher education, whether at home or abroad, is the right decision for students today. For decades, we have attracted more students from China than almost any other country in the world. This year, we have more than 62,000 Chinese students studying in the US. Today, we invite even more of you to join us. Whether you pursue a short stay or a multi-year degree program, an exchange will enrich your education experience and help you create a network of new friends and future colleagues that will last a lifetime.

Part E Fun Time

Listening Script

Directions: Listen twice to a humorous story about two people from different countries on a ship. Retell the story and point out the misunderstanding between these two people.

Mr. Goldberg, from Russia, coming to America, shared a table in the ship's dining room with a Frenchman.

The first day out, the Frenchman approached the table, bowed and said, "Bon appétit!"

Goldberg, puzzled for a moment, bowed back and replied "Goldberg."

Every day, at every meal, the same routine occurred.

On the fifth day, another passenger took Goldberg aside. "Listen, the Frenchman isn't telling you his name. He's saying 'Good Appetite,' that's what 'Bon appétit!' means."

At the next meal, Mr. Goldberg, beaming, bowed to the Frenchman and said, "Bon appétit!"

And the Frenchman, beaming, replied: "Goldberg!"

Note

Bon appétit!

This French expression means "good appetite". It is a wish for the health and happiness of someone who is about to eat or have a meal. In the story, when the Frenchman said "Bon appétit", the Russian gentleman thought he was introducing himself, so he said "Goldberg" to tell the Frenchman his own name, too, but the Frenchman thought "Goldberg" was a Russian word for "Bon appétit".

Unit 2

Personal Finances

Preview

This unit integrates various useful expressions and authentic talks about personal finances.

Objectives

After studying this unit, the students are expected to:
1. know the basic words and expressions about personal finances;
2. understand conversations and short talks about personal finances;
3. be able to give brief talks about how to handle personal finances.

Part A　Language Focus

Notes

1. **currency**

　　Currency refers to the actual money, usually coin and paper, being used in a country.

2. **mortgage**

　　Mortgage is usually a type of loan for people who want to buy a house or an apartment. In Britain people usually get a mortgage from a bank or a building society. In the US they get one from a bank or a savings and loan association. People borrow as much as 95% of the total price of the house and pay the rest themselves. Mortgages are paid back in fixed monthly payments.

3. duty-free

    Duty-free goods are sold at duty-free shops which are often found at international airports or on planes or ships at a cheaper price than usual because you do not have to pay import tax on them.

4. VAT

    VAT stands for value added tax in Britain and Europe. In the United States, this tax is called sales tax.

Part B   Authentic Conversations

Purpose

This part aims to familiarize the students with authentic conversations that can be heard in our daily life about personal finances.

Detailed Plan

1. Study the new words and expressions in *Word Bank*.
2. Do the required exercises.
3. Check the answers.
4. Listen to the conversations again. Pay special attention to the parts you didn't understand or misunderstood. You may refer to the script if necessary.

Short Conversations

Listening Script

Directions: You will hear 6 conversations between two speakers. Listen to them and answer the following questions by choosing the right options.

1. Woman: As a freshman I have no idea about how much money I am going to spend. I am always struggling to make sure my debt doesn't grow any larger.

   Man: Neither do I. I'm in no way near paying off my credit card.

   Question: What do you know about the man?

2. Man: What do you think of the course "Finance 101" you took last semester?

   Woman: Well, I signed up for the class just thinking it would be an easy class and easy credit. But then I soon realized there was a lot of real life application. And I got really interested in it.

Question: Why was the woman interested in the course "Finance 101"?

3. Man: What is your general opinion of taxes for the Americans?

   Woman: I don't think I'm paying too much tax myself. In fact my family has benefited a lot. You know, I've got five children in school instead of somebody that has one or none. They are paying more income tax to pay for my children to go to school.

   Question: What can be inferred from the conversation?

4. Man: I think people get really excited about working for themselves instead of someone else and they may not sufficiently plan for the fact that most businesses don't turn a profit right away.

   Woman: Yes, you are right. And small businesses probably get into debt by trying to get everything at once.

   Question: Why do small businesses probably get into debt?

5. Man: Your daughter Stacy is going to Princeton University and you must be shelling out some big bucks.

   Woman: Yes. It is expensive to send a youngster to school today.

   Man: Are you doing all loans?

   Woman: No. We started saving quite a long time ago. So we are well prepared. But she has got an incredible scholarship.

   Question: What kind of financial support does Stacy have for her study at Princeton University?

6. Man: Parents play an important role in letting their children know about saving and investment. It's important for them to talk about money with children.

   Woman: Right. We encourage parents to have money conversations, play the game of Monopoly, show them calculators. If a child sees that they invest a dollar and in 65 years they'll have $1 million, it really encourages them to save and invest. And you can never start too young.

   Question: What is the best time for parents to give children financial education?

Key

1. C   2. A   3. B   4. C   5. D   6. B

Notes

1. Finance 101

It is the name of a university course. 101 is a course code, indicating that this is a basic course.

2. income tax

It is a tax paid according to a person's level of income, with people on higher incomes paying higher rates of tax. It is used by the government to help pay for things like health care and education. Income taxes provide the largest single source of government revenues in most developed countries.

3. **Princeton University**

   Princeton University is a private coeducational research university located in Princeton, New Jersey, USA. It is one of the eight universities that belong to the *Ivy League*（常春藤联盟）.

4. **Monopoly**

   Monopoly（大富翁）is a very popular board game in which players use play money to buy and trade properties, with the objective of forcing opponents into bankruptcy. It has been sold since the 1930s.

Longer Conversations

Conversation One

Listening Script

Directions: You will hear a conversation between two speakers. Listen to the conversation twice and answer the questions by choosing the right options.

Woman: Hi. How are you?

Man: Very well. Thanks.

Woman: Well, I've got a question. It's about your advice for first jobs. I'm getting a salary now for the first time in my life, having finished a Ph.D. And I'm wondering what best I can do in terms of my retirement plan, to start something now that I've finally got a salary. I'm also trying to get rid a little bit of debt acquired during grad school.

Man: I think, first of all, for most new grads and first-time job possessors, I would suggest that you save and be a net saver. It may sound like an incredibly common-place statement but the reality is most people are net borrowers; and obviously, a lot of us come out of school with some debts, some student debts — the kind we like at the Motley Fool because it usually carries a lower interest rate and it was for a really good reason. And so I would encourage you, anyone listening, who's first time on a job to save five to ten percent of your salary this year.

Questions:

1. What degree did the woman get before she got her job?
2. According to the conversation, what did the woman do to support herself during her study at the graduate school?
3. What does the man think most people do in reality?
4. What advice does the man give the woman?

Key

1. B 2. C 3. A 4. A

Notes

1. **student loan**

    Student loans are loans offered to students to assist in payment of the costs of professional education. These loans are usually at a favorable rate of interest that is subsidized by the government.

2. **the Motley Fool**

    The Motley Fool is a commercial website about stocks, investing, and personal finance. This online investment *forum*（论坛）for the individual investor emerged in 1993 and the co-founders, US entrepreneurs David and Tom Gardner, became investment *gurus*（权威）of the 1990's.

Conversation Two

Listening Script

Directions: You will hear a conversation between two speakers. Listen to the conversation twice and write your answers to the questions in the space provided below.

Man: I have a lot of bills totaled up, and it's more than I make. I can't pay them all. It's a lot of money.

Woman: It's a lot of money, but it's not unmanageable. You know, the average amount of credit card debt that a person in the United States has is $35,000. So you're not in a situation that's different from anyone else. Most of the time, we grow strongest from our weakest moments. And this is your time to climb out of the debt. I know you have a dream, I mean, you have something you wanna do, right?

Man: Yes, I wanna be a massage therapist.

Woman: All right, so you know what's gonna happen? Lowermybills.com heard about your story and they stepped in. And they're gonna start off right now by giving you $1,000 just so you can get on track.

Questions:

1. What has happened to the man?
2. How much credit card debt does the average person have in the United States?
3. What does the woman encourage the man to do?
4. What is the man's dream?
5. What is the good news for the man?

Key

1. He has a lot of bills totaled up and can't pay them all.
2. $35,000.
3. To climb out of the debt instead of giving up.
4. He wants to be a massage therapist.
5. Lowermybills.com will give him $1,000 right now.

Notes

Part C Talks from Radio/TV Programs

Purpose

This part consists of exercises based on talks excerpted from radio/TV programs. The students are expected to understand such talks and get the necessary information from them.

Detailed Plan

1. Study the new words and expressions in *Word Bank*.
2. Do the exercises based on *Excerpt One* and *Excerpt Two*.
3. Check the answers.
4. Listen to the short talks again. Pay special attention to the parts you didn't understand or misunderstood. You may refer to the script if necessary.

Excerpt One

Listening Script

Directions: You will hear a short talk from a radio program. Listen to it twice and decide whether the following statements are true (T) or false (F) according to the short talk.

My parents gave me four gifts to get me financially grounded as a kid:

They taught me the difference between savings vs. investing. I lost my initial stock market investment, but I learned so much about how Wall Street functions!

They taught me money doesn't grow on trees, but there are wiser ways to earn money. You can earn money through physical labor，but you can also make money through wise investing，loans to my brother with interest，etc.

They made me work to help defray costs for my college education. It made me study harder and this also kept me from partying too much.

They taught me to establish a budget and then go shopping for my needs. I learned that I could buy a brand name，pay twice as much，or buy generic items and stretch my dollars.

Today，I'm financially quite comfortable and enjoy making monetary decisions. That's what I call being empowered for life!

Key

1. F 2. T 3. F 4. F 5. F 6. T 7. T

Note

> **Wall Street**
> This is a narrow street in the lower part of Manhattan island，New York. It is the center of New York's financial district and the center of one of the greatest financial districts in the world as well. New York Stock Exchange and many investment firms are located there.

Excerpt Two

Listening Script

Directions：You will hear a short talk from a TV program. Listen to it twice and answer the questions by choosing the right options.

O'Brien：	Clark Howard is best known for his helpful tips on how to save money and how to get good deals. Now he's got tips for parents who want to teach their kids financial responsibility. The book is called *Clark Smart Parents*，*Clark Smart Kids*. Radio talk show host，columnist and author Clark Howard joins us. Nice to talk to you. Thanks for being with us.
Clark Howard, author：	Thank you.
O'Brien：	You've got some great tips in the book. And I kind of want to run through some of them.
Howard：	Sure.
O'Brien：	First，you say deferred gratification. What exactly does that mean?
Howard：	Yes. A kid doesn't understand the idea of why they can't have something right now. Most of us as adults don't get the idea that we can't have whatever we want right this second. So the idea of delayed gratification is you start teaching a child that，OK，you can have this now，but if you wait，you're going to have more. And so I'm really big on exercises in the book，things you can try that might or might not be appropriate for your child，to get the idea that if you

	wait, you're rewarded with more later.
O'Brien:	I'm intrigued by this tip: you say keep track of credit card purchases with a checkbook register.
Howard:	Yes.
O'Brien:	I think that's so smart, because kids ...
Howard:	Adults should do this, too.
O'Brien:	Right.
Howard:	If you just use a credit card, you're not thinking about what you're spending. But if you keep a check register every purchase you make on a credit card, it changes how you spend money. You really have to think about what you're spending. Now, my 15-year-old just overdrew her account with her debit card, and she got hit with the fees. And that was a good ...
O'Brien:	Has she learned a lesson yet?
Howard:	Not yet, because this is only the second time she's overdrawn her account. But it's part of the process of her learning the logical consequences of not behaving with money.

Questions:

1. What is the title of Clark Howard's new book?
2. Who are Howard's tips intended for?
3. What does Howard mean by "deferred gratification"?
4. Why does a credit card holder need a checkbook register?
5. What can you know about Howard's daughter from what Howard has said in the talk?

Key

1. C   2. B   3. B   4. A   5. C

Note

Clark Howard

Clark Howard (born June 20, 1955), is a popular American talk radio host. He is also the author of several books on consumer tips and bargains, such as *Clark Smart Parents*, *Clark Smart Kids*, *Clark's Big Book of Bargains*, etc.

Part D   Dictation

Purpose

This part contains a short talk to be dictated to the students. This exercise trains the students' skills in

writing down what they have heard.

Detailed Plan

1. Study the new words and expressions in *Word Bank*.
2. Listen to the short talk from the beginning to the end without any pause.
3. Write down the sentences during the pauses when the short talk is spoken again.
4. Read the listening script and correct whatever mistakes the students may have made.
5. Listen to the short talk again if necessary.

Listening Script

Directions: You will hear a short talk by Ms. Mellody Hobson, a successful business woman. The short talk will be spoken twice. After you listen to it at normal speed, the short talk will be spoken again with pauses. During the pauses, write down what you hear in the space provided below.

I'm the youngest of six children. And my mom was a single mom and, like so many other single moms, worked extraordinarily hard to try to provide a good life for us. And being the youngest, I had a really interesting vantage point because my oldest sister is 25 years older than me.

And all the while I was growing up, of course, there were just constant conversations about money and money being tight and how we are going to make ends meet and sometimes not having enough money. And it really just made me committed to living a life with much more financial security. I don't think it's an accident that I ended up in the money management and mutual fund business.

Note

> **Mellody Hobson**
> Mellody Hobson (born April 3, 1969) is the president of Ariel Capital Management. She is also the Chairman of the Board of Trustees of Ariel Mutual Funds.

Part E　Fun Time

Listening Script

Directions: Listen twice to a humorous story about a millionaire who loans $5,000 from a bank. Try to retell the story to your classmates.

A man walks into a bank in New York City. He tells the loan officer that he is going to Japan on business for two weeks and needs to borrow $5,000.

The bank officer tells him that the bank will need some form of security for the loan, so the man hands over the keys to a new Ferrari parked on the street in front of the bank. He produces the title and everything checks out.

The loan officer agrees to accept the car as collateral for the loan. The bank's president and officers all enjoy a good laugh at the man for using a $250,000 Ferrari as collateral against a $5,000 loan.

One of the bank's employees then drives the Ferrari into the bank's underground garage and parks it there.

Two weeks later, the man returns, repays the $5,000 and the interest, which comes to $15.41.

The loan officer says, "Sir, we are very happy to have had your business and this transaction worked out very nicely, but we are a little puzzled. While you were away, we checked you out and found that you are a millionaire. What puzzles us is, why would you bother to borrow $5,000?".

The man replies, "Where else in New York City can I park my car for two weeks for only $15.41 and expect it to be there when I return?"

Note

Parking in New York

Parking in large cities in the United States can be very expensive. Recent statistics show that the daily parking rate in central New York exceeds $40. The 3 most expensive cities in the United States are: New York, $630/month, Boston, $460/month, and San Francisco $350/month.

Unit 3

Entertainment

Preview

This unit integrates various useful expressions and authentic talks about entertainment.

Objectives

After studying this unit, the students are expected to:
1. know the basic words and expressions about different kinds of entertainment;
2. understand conversations and short talks about entertainment;
3. be able to talk about entertainment using the words and expressions learnt in this unit.

Part A Language Focus

Notes

1. **the show business**

   The show business refers to the theater, movies, television and music as a profession or industry. It can also include the artists and performers involved.

2. **amusement, recreation**

   The word *amusement* refers to the feeling that one has when something is funny or amusing. It may also refer to a game, an activity, etc. that provides entertainment and pleasure. Recreation is something that people have for pleasure when they are not working.

3. amusement park

Amusement parks have become more and more popular these days. Usually located near a big city or in a resort area, they attract visitors who come for the day as well as families on vacation who may stay for several days. Generally these amusement parks provide various forms of recreation, including rides, shows, educational exhibits, and other activities.

4. theme park

Theme park is an outdoor entertainment center that offers rides, games, exhibitions, and shows based on one or more special ideas, or themes. The use of themes is the main difference between a theme park and a traditional amusement park.

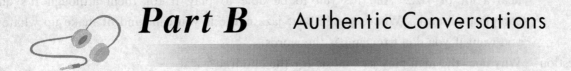

Part B Authentic Conversations

Purpose

This part aims to familiarize the students with authentic conversations that can be heard in our daily life about entertainment.

Detailed Plan

1. Study the new words and expressions in *Word Bank*.
2. Do the required exercises.
3. Check the answers.
4. Listen to the conversations again. Pay special attention to the parts you didn't understand or misunderstood. You may refer to the script if necessary.

Short Conversations

Listening Script

Directions: You will hear 6 conversations between two speakers. Listen to them and answer the following questions by choosing the right options.

1. Woman: I guess I can tell you that tonight is *Murphy Brown*. That's the one I don't miss and I don't know if you've seen that.

   Man: I have heard about it but I've never watched it. In fact I don't usually watch TV on Monday nights. I guess I'm just really tired from the weekend.

Question: What can we know about the man?

2. Man: In terms of the — in terms of the excitement, I know going to a casino, part of the reason for people to go to a casino is the people around you, the excitement, the lights. Do you think that just staring at a computer screen is not quite as exciting as actually going to a casino?

Woman: One of the things you have to keep in mind is how many people play computer games at home without the excitement of Las Vegas or anything else, just because they like to play games.

Question: What does the man think of playing computer games?

3. Woman: You're going to be performing for a bunch of children this afternoon, are you?

Man: Yes, we're playing jazz music, because, you know, a lot of kids don't get the chance to hear a lot of jazz. And it's fun to be able to play it for them although it's quite complicated music. What's good about jazz music is you can kind of make up whatever you want if you don't remember the words.

Question: Why does the man play jazz music for the children?

4. Man: My kids are involved in sports. My daughter plays basketball for 6 years and my son plays football. My rule is that they can't play a sport the same time of year.

Woman: That's why?

Man: Because there's just not enough of me to drive them around everywhere.

Question: What is the man's rule?

5. Woman: Many people this summer are opting for less expensive and closer-to-home vacations. So has that trend boosted attendance at US amusement parks?

Man: Well, the Disneyland is seeing attendance up 3 percent this year so far while other amusement parks have had a real rough time with the recession.

Question: What can we learn from the conversation?

6. Woman: Just now you let the little bird go up or under or over me somewhere over here, but I don't see it now. What happened to it?

Man: It disappeared. I'm not going to tell you any more than that, because part of the responsibility of a magician, is not to break your ability to enjoy the wonder.

Question: Why does the man refuse to tell the woman what has happened to the bird?

Key

1. D   2. A   3. A   4. B   5. C   6. D

Notes

1. Murphy Brown

Murphy Brown is an American *situation comedy*（情景喜剧）which aired on *CBS*（哥伦比亚广播公司）from November 14, 1988 to May 18, 1998, for a total of 247 episodes. In the comedy, the main character Murphy Brown is an investigative journalist and news anchor for

FYI, a fictional news magazine.

2. **casino**

This is a building or room used for gambling. Many casinos are also resort hotels, such as those in Monte Carlo, Las Vegas, and Atlantic City.

3. **Las Vegas**

Las Vegas is the largest city in Nevada, USA and a very popular tourist destination in the United States. It is famous for its hotels and gambling casinos. The city attracts about 36 million visitors a year.

4. **jazz music**

Jazz is probably the only art form of music to originate in the United States at the beginning of the twentieth century. One of the key elements of jazz is *improvisation*（即席创作）— the ability to create new music spontaneously. This skill is the distinguishing characteristic of the genuine jazz musician.

5. **Disneyland**

In 1955, a huge theme park was opened in Anaheim, California, USA. The name of the theme park Disneyland soon became well-known all over the world. After the success of the first Disney theme park, several others were built in other parts of the USA or elsewhere. In 1971, an even bigger park, Walt Disney World, opened near Orlando, Florida, USA. Other Disneyland parks have opened near Tokyo (1983), in Marne-la-Vallée, near Paris (1992), and in Hong Kong (2005).

Longer Conversations

Conversation One

Listening Script

Directions: You will hear a conversation between two speakers. Listen to the conversation twice and answer the questions by choosing the right options.

Man 1: I understand your favorite game is EverQuest.

Man 2: That's correct.

Man 1: What's the attraction? How long have you been playing?

Man 2: Well, I'm just playing the EverQuest Ⅱ actually now as I've been playing since the original EverQuest came out about 1999.

Man 1: What do you like about the game?

Man 2: I enjoy the community's people. It's a game that I allowed my kids to play. And my older son and I tend to communicate a lot of times when I'm traveling around.

Man 1: When you're on the road, how do you play? Do you have a laptop?

Man 2: Yeah, I have a laptop. Computers are kind of my hobby. Some guys have cars and stuff and that's been computers for me. So, I've always tried to keep my laptops souped up enough that I can run real comfortably playing on the road.

Man 1: I'm not gonna ask you your screen name for obvious reasons, although. But I also read that you like playing with people you might not have met otherwise online?

Man 2: Yeah, the community aspect is certainly the huge draw for an online game. And you know, there's a large consistent group of people that I play with. They know who I am and it's not a big deal for them, which makes it much more comfortable anyway for me to play. So, yeah, it's definitely the community and you know any online game has a community, but I think the biggest thing with EverQuest is the game itself and all that comes with it.

Questions:

1. What can you know about the computer game according to what the man has said?
2. Why does the man try to make his laptop more powerful all the time?
3. What does the man enjoy most about EverQuest?

Key

1. B   2. C   3. A

Notes

1. **EverQuest**

    EverQuest is an online multiplayer game released in 1999 that features over 12 different races, 14 classes, and an abundance of special skills and abilities to transform your character into a unique person in a thriving world. EverQuest II was released in late 2004.

2. **screen name**

    In a computing context, users may need to identify themselves for the purposes of security, logging and resource management. In order to identify oneself, a user has an account (a user account) and a username (also called a screen name, handle, nickname, or nick on some systems).

3. **... any online game has a community**

    Online games refer to video games that are played over some form of computer network, most commonly the Internet. Many online games have associated online communities, making online games a form of social activity beyond single player games.

Conversation Two

Listening Script

Directions: You will hear a conversation between two speakers. Listen to the conversation twice and write your answers to the questions in the space provided below.

Simon: I have read some interviews with you where you've talked, I thought I must say quite interestingly, about the particular emotional response that music can invoke in people.

Enya: Yes, I know that for some of my fans when they talk about listening to the music, firstly, they talk about their favorite song. But so many of them seem to be able to interpret their own emotions with the music. I think it's really important to have time to yourself. And a lot of people don't take this time anymore. You're caught up with work and live in very noisy environments today. So therefore, you don't get the opportunity to sort of just sit and think about life in general. But I feel that people are doing this through my music. And I think that's really healthy.

Simon: Mmm-hm. Forgive me for putting it this way, but if someone recognized you on the street, which must happen, and said to you: "C'mon, Enya, sing a song," could you do it? Would you want to do it?

Enya: No, because there's a side of me that's quite shy. What I feel with my music is that I can express myself so much. And a lot of the fans can sense that I'm relating to them something quite personal. So therefore, standing in the street singing wouldn't be something that I would be known for.

Simon: Oh, all right. Do you ever enjoy just standing around singing, maybe with your friends, and not just singing with yourself over and over again in the studio?

Enya: Oh, oh yeah.

Simon: It's been a pleasure talking to you.

Enya: Oh, thank you.

Questions:

1. Talking about interviews with the woman, what has the man found interesting?
2. What are many of the woman's fans able to do with the music?
3. Why don't people have time to themselves any more?
4. In the woman's opinion, what can people do through her music?
5. Why wouldn't the woman sing to people in the street?
6. What else does the woman enjoy doing besides singing with herself in the studio?

Key

1. The emotional response that music can invoke in people.
2. They are able to interpret their own emotions with the music.
3. Because they are caught up with work and live in very noisy environments.
4. They can get the opportunity to sit and think about life in general.
5. Because she is quite shy.
6. She also enjoys standing around singing with her friends.

Note

Enya

Born in 1961 to a musical family, Enya is an Irish singer and songwriter. She is Ireland's best-selling solo artist.

Part C   Talks from Radio/TV Programs

Purpose

This part consists of exercises based on talks excerpted from radio/TV programs. The students are expected to understand such talks and get the necessary information from them.

Detailed Plan

1. Study the new words and expressions in *Word Bank*.
2. Do the exercises based on *Excerpt One* and *Excerpt Two*.
3. Check the answers.
4. Listen to the short talks again. Pay special attention to the parts you didn't understand or misunderstood. You may refer to the script if necessary.

Excerpt One

Listening Script

Directions: You will hear a short talk from a radio program. Listen to it twice and decide whether the following statements are true (T) or false (F) according to the short talk.

Debbie Elliott, host:	There are other runners who turn marathons into an even more extreme sport. How about juggling for almost the entire course? Michal Kapral and Zach Warren are the two favorite runners in the so-called joggler division in tomorrow's Boston Marathon. Yes, jogglers.
	Michal Kapral set a world record as a joggler, and Zach Warren is the young whippersnapper who stole the title. They meet for the first time tomorrow. We have them on the line now. Welcome, gentlemen.
Unidentified Man #1:	Thanks, hi.
Unidentified Man #2:	Hey, Debbie, thanks.
Elliott:	So we'll start with you, Michal. Joggling?
Mr. Michal Kapral (Marathon Joggler):	Yeah, joggling. I read about it way back when my sister and I used to flip through the *Guinness Book of World Records*, about 20 years ago. Somehow it stuck in my head, and here I am, the joggler.
Elliott:	Is there a special technique to this?
Mr. Kapral:	For me it took a while to learn because I'm not a natural juggler. I knew how to juggle,

but I'd only done it for maybe three minutes, max, and pushing that to three hours for me was a big jump, and it took me about a month of practice at about four in the morning so no one would see me dropping balls all over the place.

Elliott: So, Zach, what do you do if you drop a ball during the race?

Mr. Zach Warren (Marathon Joggler): Every time you drop the ball, you have to go back and pick it up, so obviously a key strategy is not to drop the ball.

Key

1. F 2. F 3. T 4. T 5. T 6. F 7. T

Notes

1. marathon

A marathon is a race in which runners run over land, including city streets, covering a distance of exactly 26 miles and 385 yards (42.2 kilometers).

The marathon's name comes from a place called Marathon in Greece. According to legend, in 490 BC, Pheidippides, a runner from Marathon, carried news of victory over the *Persians*(波斯人) to *Athens*(雅典).

The marathon is one of the Olympic running events. Many cities in the world also host their marathons. The best-known marathons in the United States are the Boston Marathon and the New York City Marathon.

2. joggler

A joggler is a person who jogs or runs while juggling. In English, jog means "to run slowly and steadily for a long time" and juggle means "to keep three or more objects moving through the air by throwing and catching them very quickly". The joggler is a person who does these two things at the same time.

Excerpt Two

Listening Script

Directions: You will hear a short talk from a TV program. Listen to it twice and answer the questions by choosing the right options.

Man: Time for the shot of the day. We could not resist this video. It's a cute odd couple, a dog and a duck. There you go.

Woman: Oh, look at that!

Man: Sure. They've become best friends in China. A girl apparently got the duck as a gift to play with, and her dad found the abandoned puppy, brought it home.

Woman: Oh, sweet.

Man: And the dog and the duck have been by each (other) — look at that — ever since.

Woman: That is too cute.

Man: I know.

Woman：Oh，look，and the duck is sort of just giving him little kisses.

Man：Isn't that sweet?

Woman：I love it. That is a good video.

Man：I know. And when the duck is slaughtered for food，the dog is going to like her even more.

Woman：That's horrible.

Man：What?

Woman：That is awful. I thought you were a friend of the animals. I thought you liked ducks and puppies.

Man：I love ducks and puppies. What do you think is going to happen to that duck?

Woman：What? I hope it doesn't become food. I'm not going to eat the duck，I'll tell you that.

Man：You're right.

Woman：Have a great weekend.

Man：Thanks，you，too. I'm going to get e-mails. We want you to send us your shot ideas. If you see some amazing video，tell us about it.

Questions：

1. What is so cute in the video according to the woman?
2. When will the dog love the duck even more according to the man?
3. What does the man hate according to the woman?
4. What does the woman hope while talking about what's going to happen to the duck?
5. What does the man invite the viewers to do at the end of the video?

Key

1. C 2. B 3. A 4. D 5. D

Notes

1. And the dog and the duck have been by each (other) . . .

In this sentence，*have been by each other* means "have stayed side by side". The word "other" cannot be heard because the speaker sees something interesting and stops to invite the woman to look at it.

2. shot ideas

This conversation is taken from a program called *Anderson Cooper 360 Degrees* aired on CNN. The section you have heard is called "the Shot of the Day"，meaning the picture or video that is worth seeing for the day. In this context，"shot ideas" refers to good ideas about videos or pictures worth seeing.

Part D   Dictation

Purpose

This part contains a short talk to be dictated to the students. This exercise trains the students' skills in writing down what they have heard.

Detailed Plan

1. Study the new words and expressions in *Word Bank*.
2. Listen to the short talk from the beginning to the end without any pause.
3. Write down the sentences during the pauses when the short talk is spoken again.
4. Read the listening script and correct whatever mistakes the students may have made.
5. Listen to the short talk again if necessary.

Listening Script

Directions: You will hear a short talk about Disneyland. The short talk will be spoken twice. After you listen to it at normal speed, the short talk will be spoken again with pauses. During the pauses, write down what you hear in the space provided below.

In 1955 Walt Disney opened an amusement park not far from Hollywood, California. He called it "Disneyland". He wanted it to be the happiest place on Earth.

Disneyland recreated imaginary places from Disney movies. It also recreated real places as Disney imagined them. For example, one area looked like a 19th century town in the American West. Another looked like the world of the future.

Disneyland also had exciting rides. Children could fly on an elephant or climb a mountain or float on a jungle river. And — best of all — children got to meet Mickey Mouse himself. Actors dressed as Mickey and all the Disney cartoon creatures walked around the park shaking hands.

Notes

1. **Walt Disney**

   Walt Disney (1901—1966) was one of the most famous motion-picture producers in history. Disney first became known in the 1920's and 1930's for creating such cartoon film characters as Mickey Mouse and Donald Duck. Disney won 32 *Academy Awards* (奥斯卡奖) for his movies and for scientific and technical contributions to filmmaking. He also gained fame for his development of theme parks.

2. Hollywood

   Hollywood is generally considered the motion-picture capital of the world. It is a district of Los Angeles, USA. It became the center of the movie industry by 1915. Today it is a popular destination for nightlife and tourism and home to many entertainment-related companies.

3. Mickey Mouse

   Mickey Mouse is a comic animal cartoon character who has become an *icon*（象征）for The Walt Disney Company. Mickey Mouse was created in 1928 by Walt Disney.

Part E Fun Time

Listening Script

Directions: Listen twice to a humorous story about a parrot and a magician. Retell the story and discuss with your classmates what answer might be expected from the magician in the sea.

   A magician was working on a cruise ship in the ocean. The audience would be different each week, so the magician allowed himself to do the same tricks over and over again. There was only one problem: The captain's parrot saw the shows every week and began to understand what the magician did in every trick. Once he understood that, he started shouting in the middle of the show: "Look, it's not the same hat!" "Look, he's hiding the flowers under the table!" The magician was furious but couldn't do anything. It was the captain's parrot after all.

   One day the ship had an accident and sank. The magician found himself on a piece of wood in the middle of the ocean, and of course the parrot was by his side. They stared at each other with hate, but did not utter a word. This went on for several days. After a week the parrot finally said: "Okay, I give up. What did you do with the boat?"

Unit 4

Sympathy and Consolation

Preview

This unit integrates various useful expressions and authentic talks about sympathy and consolation.

Objectives

After studying this unit, the students are expected to:
1. know the basic words and expressions about sympathy and consolation;
2. understand conversations and short talks about different ways to express sympathy and consolation;
3. be able to express sympathy and consolation.

Part A   Language Focus

Notes

1. **feeling, sense**

   Feeling is a general term for an emotion that comes through the mind or through the senses.

   e.g. It was a wonderful feeling to be home again.

   Sense is a feeling that comes from various sense impressions, usually about something worthy of one's attention.

   e.g. a sense of loss, a sense of relief

2. **be in a bad mood**

   The phrase means feel unhappy or angry.

e.g. He lost his wallet and was in a bad mood today.

3. be in low spirits

The phrase means be unhappy or depressed.

e.g. The family were in low spirits after the earthquake.

4. What a shame!

The word *shame*, as the word *pity*, can be used when you wish a situation was different, and you feel sad or disappointed.

e.g. "Tom's failed his test again." "What a shame!"

It's a shame that we missed the train because of the traffic jam.

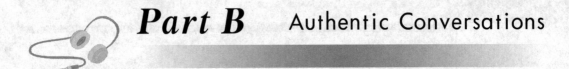

Part B   Authentic Conversations

Purpose

This part aims to familiarize the students with authentic conversations that can be heard in our daily life about sympathy and consolation.

Detailed Plan

1. Study the new words and expressions in *Word Bank*.
2. Do the required exercises.
3. Check the answers.
4. Listen to the conversations again. Pay special attention to the parts you didn't understand or misunderstood. You may refer to the script if necessary.

Short Conversations

Listening Script

Directions: You will hear 6 conversations between two speakers. Listen to them and answer the following questions by choosing the right options.

1. Woman: About what time did the tornado hit your town?

   Man: I think it must have been about 7:30.

   Woman: Were you still at your business?

   Man: Yes, almost everyone from the town came to our restaurant. It's cement block, and I think they felt that it was the safest place to go. People were here until midnight.

Question: Why did everyone come to the man's restaurant when the tornado hit the town?

2. Man: It's been almost a year since your husband and son's accident. Are you able to think about them without feeling great sorrow?

Woman: I think about them every day, of course. However time will heal and life will go on.

Question: Which of the following is true about the woman?

3. Man: I am so sorry for what you and your family have been through. It breaks my heart when you tell the tragic story of your sister. How are you holding up now?

Woman: Pretty good. We are very grateful for all the love and support we have received from the people here since the worst thing that ever happened to us.

Question: What can you conclude from the conversation?

4. Woman: I'd like to express my sympathy to a co-worker whose father recently passed away. What's the best way to convey my condolences?

Man: Offering sympathy can feel uncomfortable, but even the clumsiest attempt is better than not acknowledging a loss.

Question: In the man's opinion, what should the woman do?

5. Woman: How do you survive Thanksgiving?

Man: Well, I just stay indoors with the doors locked.

Woman: So you survive Thanksgiving by basically ignoring it.

Man: Well, you see, everybody takes pity on me. I am the object of pity for a few days, because everybody thinks he's in a foreign country, we should feel sorry for him. Why do you think I'm in a foreign country? To escape my family.

Question: What can you know about the man from this conversation?

6. Man: I know that one of your most often-requested columns is about grief.

Woman: Right.

Man: Are you amazed that people still are so hungry for — for comfort and for consoling words?

Woman: Not at all. I've found that people do often feel alone, and they need the sense of connection.

Question: Why is the column about grief often requested?

Key

1. B 2. A 3. D 4. C 5. C 6. A

Note

column

A column is a regular section of a newspaper or magazine on a particular subject or by a particular person. The writer of the articles for this section is called a columnist.

Longer Conversations

Conversation One

Listening Script

Directions: You will hear a conversation between two speakers. Listen to the conversation twice and answer the questions by choosing the right options.

Man: I heard that a tornado killed at least three people and injured at least eight others in your hometown. How about your home?

Woman: Our home is fine. We're fine, but my close friends have lost homes and farms. Two of the deaths are our regular customers and very good friends of my husband's.

Man: I'm sorry to hear that. Can you tell me right now how the town is trying to recover today? Is your phone service working pretty well right now?

Woman: We're fine, but within a couple of miles, they have no electricity, no telephones, nothing. Everyone is trying to help.

Man: Do you think you have got enough help there? Have you seen the Red Cross out there or anything?

Woman: I haven't seen the Red Cross here yet. I know our local volunteer fire department has been working since 8:00 last night, looking for missing people. As far as I know, everyone has been accounted for.

Questions:

1. What is the main topic of this conversation?
2. Who have lost homes and farms?
3. What is true about the town after the disaster?

Key

1. D   2. A   3. D

Notes

1. **Red Cross**

   The name Red Cross generally refers to the *humanitarian*（慈善的）organization, the International Committee of the Red Cross, founded in 1863 in Geneva, Switzerland. It works to relieve suffering caused by wars and natural disasters. The symbol of the Red Cross is a red cross on a white background.

2. **fire department**

   In Britain, the name "fire brigade" is used instead of the American name "fire department". It is an organization of people who are trained and employed to put out fires and to rescue people from fires and other dangerous situations.

Conversation Two

Listening Script

Directions: You will hear a conversation between two speakers. Listen to the conversation twice and write your answers to the questions in the space provided below.

Caller: How you are doing, Mrs. Reeve?

Mrs. Reeve: Hi.

Caller: I just wanted to say, I saw you on *Oprah Winfrey* two weeks ago. And, man, I wish that I could have been there to let you know how much your husband meant to me. I broke my neck in 1998. And like your husband, I didn't — initially, I wanted to commit suicide but, because I saw what he went through and how he handled it, it gave me the strength and the courage to continue to do the things that I needed to do to support my wife and kids. And I just wanted to let you know that, if there is anything that I can do to assist the Christopher Reeve Foundation, let me know, if it's just as small as licking envelopes and just mailing things out. I mean ...

Mrs. Reeve: Great.

Caller: Where can I go to find out information about how I can just help with the organization?

Mrs. Reeve: What you should do is call our resource center. It's the Christopher and Dana Reeve Paralysis Resource Center. You sound like you'd be great. I'm so happy to hear, and Chris would be so happy to know, that he affected you in such a way. Because he really did on a regular basis reach out to people.

Questions:

1. Where did the man see the woman two weeks ago?
2. What happened to the man in 1998?
3. What did the man want to do after his tragic accident?
4. Why did the man give up his suicide attempt later?
5. What did the man want to do for the Christopher Reeve Foundation?
6. How can the man get information about the Christopher Reeve Foundation?
7. Who would be happy to know what the man has said?

Key

1. On TV.
2. He broke his neck.
3. He wanted to commit suicide.
4. Because Christopher Reeve set a good example for him.
5. He was ready to do anything.
6. He should call the Christopher and Dana Reeve Paralysis Resource Center.
7. Christopher Reeve.

Notes

1. caller

This conversation is excerpt from a TV talk show. After talking to the TV host, Mrs. Reeve is taking phone calls from the viewers.

2. Mrs. Reeve

Mrs. Reeve is the wife of the famous American actor Christopher Reeve, who starred in four popular motion pictures based on the well-known Superman stories. Christopher Reeve was paralyzed from the neck down in a horseback riding accident in 1995.

3. Christopher Reeve Foundation

The Christopher and Dana Reeve Foundation (CDRF) is a charitable organization dedicated to finding treatments and cures for paralysis caused by *spinal cord* (脊髓) injury and other *neurological* (神经的) disorders. It also works to improve the quality of life for people living with disabilities.

4. the Christopher and Dana Reeve Paralysis Resource Center

The Paralysis Resource Center is a program created by the Christopher and Dana Reeve Foundation to provide a comprehensive, national source of information for people living with paralysis and their *caregivers* (护理者).

 Part C   Talks from TV Programs

Purpose

This part consists of exercises based on talks excerpted from TV programs. The students are expected to understand such talks and get the necessary information from them.

Detailed Plan

1. Study the new words and expressions in *Word Bank*.
2. Do the exercises based on *Excerpt One* and *Excerpt Two*.
3. Check the answers.
4. Listen to the short talks again. Pay special attention to the parts you didn't understand or misunderstood. You may refer to the script if necessary.

Excerpt One

Listening Script

Directions: You will hear a short talk from a TV program. Listen to it twice and write your answers to the questions in the space provided below.

I'm Governor Bill Owens, and I thank you for gathering with us this afternoon.

We're here to pay tribute to the slain victims of the Columbine High School tragedy. As I look out on these thousands of faces, I see through the grief and the tears an outpouring of love. Faced with an astonishing evil, you have come together to offer support and comfort to each other.

Since the terrible events of Tuesday, we've seen a community that has found within itself a great healing power. On behalf of all the citizens of Colorado, I extend my deep, heart-felt sorrow and sympathy to the students, faculty and families of Columbine High School. At a time like this it is very difficult to find the right words, but sometimes words aren't even necessary. When one of his classmates died, an eight-year-old friend visited the deceased boy's home one afternoon after school. "What did you say?" asked his mother gently when the child returned home. "Nothing, I just sat on his mom's lap and cried with her."

Well, today we stand shoulder to shoulder to cry with you; to share your grief and to offer you our love. To the law enforcement officers, to the doctors and nurses, to the teachers and students, to the citizen volunteers — the thousands of citizen volunteers thank you for coming to the aid of our community.

Questions:

1. Who is the speaker?
2. What kind of tragedy has taken place at Columbine High School?
3. According to the speaker, what have people come to offer this afternoon?
4. What kind of feeling does the speaker want to extend to the people at Columbine High School?
5. What did an eight-year-old boy do to comfort his deceased friend's mom?
6. What does the governor say to all the people who have offered their help?

Key

1. Governor Bill Owens.
2. Some people have been killed.
3. Support and comfort to each other.
4. Heart-felt sorrow and sympathy.
5. He just sat on her lap and cried with her.
6. He says "thank you" to all people.

Notes

1. **Colorado**

It is a state located in the Rocky Mountain region of the United States. Denver is the capital as well as the most populous city of Colorado.

2. Columbine High School

It is a secondary school in Jefferson County, Colorado. Columbine High School was the site of the fourth deadliest school massacre in modern United States history. The school shooting took place on April 20, 1999, when Eric Harris and Dylan Klebold killed 12 students and one teacher, and wounded 24 others, before taking their own lives. The massacre made headlines around the world, making Columbine a household name, and causing a moral panic in American high schools.

3. law enforcement officers

Law enforcement officers are people charged with keeping the law and peace, including police officers, customs officers, *correctional* (惩教的) officers, etc.

Excerpt Two

Listening Script

Directions: You will hear a short talk from a TV program. Listen to it twice and answer the questions by choosing the right options.

Celine Dion:

I'm waking up in the morning. I'm having a coffee. I barely can swallow it. I come here at Caesar's Palace every night to perform. I barely can sing. But for respect for the people who come I am still singing. When I come home at night, my son is waiting for me. I watch television.

Yes, we gave $1 million but what we expect, what I want to look like the rest of the world, I open the television there's people still there waiting to be rescued and for me it's not acceptable. I know there's reasons for it. I'm sorry to say I'm being rude but I don't want to hear those reasons.

You know, some people are stealing and they're making a big deal out of it. Oh, they're stealing 20 pairs of jeans or they're stealing television sets. Who cares? They're not going to go too far with it.

The main thing right now it's not the people who are stealing. It's the people who are left there and they're watching helicopters flying over their heads and they're praying. How come it's so easy to send planes in another country to kill everyone in a second, to destroy lives?

We need to serve our country and for me to serve our country is to be there right now to rescue the rest of the people. We need the cash. We need the blood. We need the support. Right now we need the prayers.

It is ... You know when I was hearing a couple of days ago that these things are not reachable it's too full of water, maybe I'm too much like my — I'm not thinking with my head. I'm talking with my heart. Nobody can open any roofs? The helicopters flying in take two people at a time, take a kayak. Go into those walls.

There's kids being raped at night. They hear gunshots, big guns, what's that? Those people are praying. They're walking. They're like this, hello, do you see us? We're still alive but we're dying. It's terrible.

Questions：

1. Why is the speaker so upset?
2. What does the speaker say is unacceptable?
3. What is the most urgent thing to do right now according to the speaker?
4. What does the speaker suggest to the rescuers?
5. Which of the following is not mentioned in the speaker's description of the flooded area?

Key

1. D 2. A 3. A 4. B 5. D

Notes

1. **Celine Dion**

    Celine Dion is a French-Canadian singing star. She first gained recognition in Canada and spoke and performed only in French until she learned English in 1989. She achieved great success through her English-language recordings.

    In this talk，Celine Dion is being interviewed by CNN's famous host Larry King about *Hurricane Katrina*（卡特里娜飓风）that hit the United States in August of 2005. At least 1,836 people lost their lives in Hurricane Katrina and in the subsequent floods.

2. **Caesar's Palace**

    This is a Roman-themed hotel offering luxurious *amenities*（令人愉快之事物）in Las Vegas，a major tourist center known for its casinos. It took 4 years（from 1962 to 1966）to build the hotel，which opened on August 5，1966.

3. **we gave $1 million**

    Celine Dion donated $1 million to help the flood victims.

4. **there's people ...**

    Grammatically，one should say "there are people".

5. **there's reasons ...**

    Grammatically，one should say "there are reasons".

6. **How come it's so easy to send planes in another country to kill everyone in a second, to destroy lives?**

    Here Celine Dion is referring to the Iraq War that began in March 2003 when the United States and its allies launched an invasion of Iraq.

Part D Dictation

Purpose

This part contains a short talk to be dictated to the students. This exercise trains the students' skills in writing down what they have heard.

Detailed Plan

1. Study the new words and expressions in *Word Bank*.
2. Listen to the short talk from the beginning to the end without any pause.
3. Write down the sentences during the pauses when the short talk is spoken again.
4. Read the listening script and correct whatever mistakes the students may have made.
5. Listen to the short talk again if necessary.

Listening Script

Directions: You will hear a short talk given by Matt's family. The short talk will be spoken twice. After you listen to it at normal speed, the short talk will be spoken again with pauses. During the pauses, write down what you hear in the space provided below.

How do you deal with grief? Well, I'm learning. I think after Chris's accident, there was a sense of loss, but we were able to share it. And I'm finding that now, really, what you need to do is, you need to turn to family and you need to turn to friends and you need to truly have the person inhabit you. And I feel like that has happened.

I also believe the only cure for grief is grieving. You really need to let it come up, and gradually, you have a feeling that — you know, you start feeling OK.

Note

> **Mrs. Reeve**
>
> Please see Notes for Conversation Two of Longer Conversations, Part B of this Unit.

Part E Fun Time

Listening Script

Directions: Listen to a poem entitled *Sympathy* written by Emily Brontë. Tell what Emily Brontë thought of people's miseries and despair in the poem.

Sympathy

Emily Brontë

There should be no despair for you

While nightly stars are burning;

While evening pours its silent dew

And sunshine gilds the morning.

There should be no despair — though tears
May flow down like a river:
Are not the best beloved of years
Around your heart for ever?

They weep, you weep, it must be so;
Winds sigh as you are sighing,
And Winter sheds its grief in snow
Where Autumn's leaves are lying:
Yet, these revive, and from their fate
Your fate cannot be parted:
Then, journey on, if not elate,
Still *never* broken-hearted!

Notes

Emily Brontë

Emily Brontë (July 30, 1818—December 19, 1848) was a British novelist and poet. In her life, she produced but one novel, *Wuthering Heights* (1847), and some well-known poems.

Are not the best beloved of years
Around your heart for ever?

Through this question, the poet reminds us that the best things in our life still stay near us.

They weep, you weep, it must be so;

In this line, the pronoun "They" refers to the objects in nature as described in the poem.

. . . and from their fate
Your fate cannot be parted

The normal sentence order would be "Your fate cannot be parted from their fate." In other words, as everything in nature can revive, so can you.

Then, journey on

In this line, the word "journey" is used as a verb, meaning "go."

Hometown

Preview

This unit integrates various useful expressions and authentic talks about hometown.

Objectives

After studying this unit, the students are expected to:
1. know the basic words and expressions that are needed to talk about hometown;
2. understand conversations and short talks about people's hometown;
3. be able to talk about their own hometown.

Part A Language Focus

Notes

1. **ground/first/second floor (*BrE*), first floor/second/third floor (*AmE*)**

    In British English, the floor of a building that is at the same level as the ground outside is called the "ground floor", but in American English, it is called the "first floor". The floor immediately above the ground floor is "the first floor" in British English, but in American English, it is the second floor. This difference goes on to all the other levels of a building.

2. **Maglev**

    Maglev or magnetic levitation is an electrically operated high-speed train that goes above a track by means of a magnetic field. The magnets provide support without contact or *friction* (摩擦), allowing for fast, quiet operation.

Part B   Authentic Conversations

Purpose

This part aims to familiarize the students with authentic conversations that can be heard in our daily life about hometown.

Detailed Plan

1. Study the new words and expressions in *Word Bank*.
2. Do the required exercises.
3. Check the answers.
4. Listen to the conversations again. Pay special attention to the parts you didn't understand or misunderstood. You may refer to the script if necessary.

Short Conversations

Listening Script

Directions: You will hear 6 conversations between two speakers. Listen to them and answer the following questions by choosing the right options.

1. Man: Hi, Lesley. It seems that you are not local. Where are you from?
   Woman: I was born in Arkansas and raised in Virginia. I studied at Harvard University in Boston. Since graduation I have been working here in the New York Stock Exchange.
   Question: Where was the woman born?

2. Man: Hi, Mary. I am thinking of buying a house. Any suggestion? How about your neighbourhood?
   Woman: Well, we moved into this house last year. It's in one of the older areas of the town. One thing I really like is that it has big trees everywhere. You know lots of shade, squirrels and birds. It's really pretty. But the house is really small.
   Question: Which of the following is not true about the woman's house?

3. Man: It has been a decade since I left my hometown. What's going on there?
   Woman: Industries have sprung up, such as coal mines, chemical plants, and power plants. And people's living conditions are getting much better. Some families can even afford cars.

Question: Which of the following is not included in the industries of the man's hometown?

4. Man: My shop is located in the downtown pedestrian zone and I'm sure it will make profits soon. Moving to a new place, I may not have such a good opportunity again.

   Woman: But the living conditions in Shanghai are much better than in our hometown.

   Man: You are right. But I won't see my relatives and neighbors anymore. I will spend a lot of time adjusting to the new environment.

   Question: What kind of feeling does the man show while talking to the woman?

5. Man: Many changes have taken place in our hometown. But some problems have also arisen.

   Woman: Yes, I think our major problem is air quality. People have this love affair with their automobile here. They believe that mass transit isn't needed. They vote it down every time.

   Question: Why is there no mass transit in the speakers' hometown?

6. Woman: Once upon a time the only foreign accents heard in these malls in Arlington came from French and Spanish classes.

   Man: That's history. Today in Arlington, one in five residents is foreign-born. And in the public schools, one in four students speaks English as a second language. And countywide, white students are now in the minority.

   Question: According to the conversation, what changes have taken place in Arlington today?

Key

1. C   2. D   3. A   4. B   5. B   6. A

Notes

1. Arkansas

Arkansas is a state located in the southern region of the United States. The capital and most populous city is Little Rock. Its natural features include Hot Springs National Park and the only diamond mine in America.

2. Virginia

Virginia is an American state on the Atlantic Coast of the Southern United States. Its capital city is Richmond. It was the first permanent English colony in North America and was named after the Virgin Queen, Elizabeth I (1533—1603, the queen of England from 1558 until her death).

3. New York Stock Exchange

New York Stock Exchange (NYSE) is the largest stock exchange in the US, where shares in companies are bought and sold. It is also called "the Big Board" and its building is on Wall Street in New York City.

4. Arlington

Arlington County is an urban county of about 206,800 residents in Virginia. It is located directly across the Potomac River from Washington, D.C. It is the site of *Arlington National Cemetery* (阿林顿国家公墓).

Longer Conversations

Conversation One

Listening Script

Directions: You will hear a conversation between two speakers. Listen to the conversation twice and answer the questions by choosing the right options.

Man: Point Pleasant Beach is a great town to grow up in. Families come here and they stay. You know, it's kind of a unique place. It hasn't really changed in 25 years. I don't think it ever will, Lindy.

Woman: You are right. Its character hasn't changed since the 1880s when the railroad started carrying beachgoers here from New York. Today Pont Pleasant Beach retains that small town feel. No neon signs or fast food joints anywhere along Arnold Avenue.

Man: Yeah, people want to be in a small town and like that atmosphere. It's being able to say hello to someone and wave to them.

Woman: And the beach has always been at the center of this town. I grew up on these beaches — learned to swim, surf, worked as a lifeguard. My kids have grown up on these beaches. But in a town where very little has changed, one of the things that's always changing is the beach. All up and down this coastline, the beaches are constantly under assault. We can see the serious consequences of beach erosion here. It's expensive to maintain the shore and getting government funding is always a battle.

Questions:

1. What does the man think of Point Pleasant Beach?
2. How did the first beachgoers come to the town in the 1880s?
3. What made people want to live in Point Pleasant Beach?
4. What is changing all the time according to the conversation?
5. What does the woman mean at the end of the conversation?

Key

1. A 2. C 3. C 4. D 5. B

Notes

1. **Point Pleasant Beach**

   Point Pleasant Beach is a *borough*（自治村镇）in Ocean County, New Jersey, United States. It was ranked the eighth best beach in New Jersey in the 2008 Top Beaches *sponsored*（发起）by the New Jersey Marine Sciences *Consortium*（社会）.

2. ... **since the 1880s when the railroad started carrying beachgoers here from New York.**

A vast system of railroads began to develop in the US from the 1820s. In the 1860s, twenty-two thousand miles of new track were laid. In the following decade, forty thousand miles of new rail lines were built. In the 1880s, more than seven thousand miles of new rail line were laid. By the end of the nineteenth century, railroads in the US were carrying passengers and goods all over the country across great distances.

Conversation Two

Listening Script

Directions: You will hear a conversation between two speakers. Listen to the conversation twice and write your answers to the questions in the space provided below.

Man: Many personal stories reflect recent changes in American life. Small towns in this country are fighting many battles.

Woman: Yes, my hometown is no different.

Man: I remember thirty years ago this street was filled with family-owned businesses. But then came the malls. Many of the shoppers left, many of the stores had to close. It's been a struggle, but you are surviving.

Woman: Yeah. I have a clothing store downtown. I'm competing against four malls within a 20-mile radius of my door. It's a tremendous struggle. Every single day, every single minute in this store is a struggle. We can't compete with the pricing, the sales, the hours, and all that kind of thing. All we can compete with is the feeling. We have a feeling that you can't get at the mall. And that feeling goes a long way.

Questions:

1. What was the street like thirty years ago?
2. Why did many of the shoppers leave?
3. What kind of shop does the woman have?
4. Where is the woman's shop located?
5. How many malls does the woman have to compete against?
6. What are the advantages of the malls according to the conversation?
7. What is the strength of the woman's store?

Key

1. The street was filled with family-owned businesses.
2. Because the malls were opened up in the town.
3. She has a clothing store.
4. It is located in the center of the town.
5. Four.

6. The pricing, the sales, the hours, and all that kind of thing.
7. There is a feeling that people can't get at the mall.

Notes

> **1. Mall**
>
> A mall, also called shopping mall, is a large building or covered area that has many shops, restaurants, etc. inside it. A mall may also have its own parking space, banks and other services.
>
> **2. And that feeling goes a long way.**
>
> This refers to the feeling that exists in a small local shop where the shop owner and the customers all know each other. They may have a good chat when they see each other.

Part C   Talks from TV Programs

Purpose

This part consists of exercises based on talks excerpted from TV programs. The students are expected to understand such talks and get the necessary information from them.

Detailed Plan

1. Study the new words and expressions in *Word Bank*.
2. Do the exercises based on *Excerpt One* and *Excerpt Two*.
3. Check the answers.
4. Listen to the short talks again. Pay special attention to the parts you didn't understand or misunderstood. You may refer to the script if necessary.

Excerpt One

Listening Script

Directions: You will hear a short talk from a TV program. Listen to it twice and decide whether the following statements are true (T) or false (F) according to the short talk.

Brian Williams, anchor:
    When I went home to Middletown last week, I found times have changed the place.

You can see New York City from Middletown, New Jersey, but it never really felt like we were all that close. The town I knew was small, where people knew their neighbors, where it meant something to be part of it. I remember using the word "quiet" to describe it, but that was 20 years ago. That was before New York grew out from the center — the two decades of urban sprawl that suddenly gobbled up Middletown and made it a New York suburb. It's become a bedroom community where, for an increasing number of residents, Middletown is the place where they sleep between trips to the city — trips by train, car and boat — and back again.

You start saying things you never thought you'd hear yourself say, like "This used to be a farm," and "This was an open field." "This was the apple orchard near my house," and "There didn't used to be this much traffic."

You also remember that 20 years ago, as far as we were concerned, there was no better place to grow up. And so, in 1977, as a young man in a town where a lot of young men were choosing between police officer and firefighter, I chose firefighter. It was a good deal. During the process, I learned a lot about camaraderie about my town, and I learned a lot about hard work.

Key

1. F 2. T 3. T 4. F 5. T 6. T 7. T 8. F

Notes

1. **Brian Williams**

   Brian Douglas Williams (born May 5, 1959) is an American anchor and managing editor of *NBC*（全国广播公司）Nightly News, the *flagship*（旗舰，王牌）evening news program of the NBC television network.

2. **Middletown**

   Middletown is one of the oldest sites of European *settlement*（殖民）in New Jersey.

3. ... **where it meant something to be part of it.**

   "To be part of it" means "to be a member of the community" or "be part of the town's life".

4. ... **choosing between police officer and firefighter**

   The young men were faced with a choice of becoming either a police officer or a firefighter.

Excerpt Two

Listening Script

Directions: You will hear a short talk from a TV program. Listen to it twice and write your answers to the questions in the space provided below.

Stan Grant, CNN correspondent (voice-over): They call them astronauts. These astronauts land in China's big cities, Beijing or Shanghai.

David Zweig, sociologist: They're walking on two legs, as the Chinese used to say, one leg in China, one leg back in the West.

Grant: The astronauts are among tens of thousands of Chinese living abroad now going home each year. Why astronauts? Because they leave their families behind to seek riches in China's stellar economy. Sociologist David Zweig has been charting the course. He's writing a book about China's returnees.

Zweig: People back in 1989, '90, '91 and talking about going back to China, they would have said, no way they would go back. But that's a long time ago.

Grant: Dawn Zhao is going back. She left Beijing in 1989. Now in Hong Kong, she's planning a move to Shanghai. China is more energetic, she says, and it is changing. She believes she can make a difference.

Dawn Zhao, resident of Hong Kong: No matter, you know, where I go and where I have been and what passport I hold, at heart, I'm still Chinese.

Grant (on camera): As the world's factory, China manufactures everything, from electronics to clothes. And whatever China makes, the rest of the world buys.

Some economists caution, China's phenomenal growth cannot continue indefinitely. Others, though, say that, within a generation, China's economy will top America's.

For China's astronauts, it seems, as far as they're concerned, the sky is the limit.

Questions:

1. What do the Chinese living abroad call themselves when they return to their homeland?
2. What does "walking on two legs" mean in this talk?
3. Why do the Chinese returnees want to return to China according to the talk?
4. Where did the returnees want to stay around 1990?
5. Where does Dawn Zhao want to go now?
6. What do economists think of China's economy?
7. What are the prospects for China's astronauts according to the reporter?

Key

1. Astronauts.
2. It means "staying both in China and in the West."
3. Because they want to go back to China to seek riches.
4. They wanted to stay abroad.
5. She wants to go to Shanghai.
6. They have different opinions. (or: Some think China's economy will not grow forever while others think China's economy will top America's within a generation.)
7. The prospects are limitless.

Notes

1. **Stan Grant**

   Stan Grant (1963—) is an Australian journalist. He also works for CNN International, reporting news about China.

2. **walking on two legs**

   "Walking on two legs" was a policy adopted by the Chinese Communist Party for many years. It means that we need to take care of the relationship between two sides of whatever we do.

3. the sky is the limit

    Just as the sky seems infinite, this phrase basically means that there is no limit.

    e.g. *The sky is the limit to what professional athletes can earn.*

        Pick out whatever you want — the sky's the limit.

Part D   Dictation

Purpose

This part contains a short talk to be dictated to the students. This exercise trains the students' skills in writing down what they have heard.

Detailed Plan

1. Study the new words and expressions in *Word Bank*.
2. Listen to the short talk from the beginning to the end without any pause.
3. Write down the sentences during the pauses when the short talk is spoken again.
4. Read the listening script and correct whatever mistakes the students may have made.
5. Listen to the short talk again if necessary.

Listening Script

Directions: You will hear a short talk about the speaker's hometown. The short talk will be spoken twice. After you listen to it at normal speed, the short talk will be spoken again with pauses. During the pauses, write down what you hear in the space provided below.

    I grew up in four different hometowns, but I chose to go back to Greenwich, Connecticut, because that's where I went to high school. Greenwich is a town, 28 miles north of New York City. It is quiet and its reputation is based on the wealth of its residents. The town's per capita income is \$72,000 a year. The average price of home is half a million dollars. Schools here spend more than \$10,000 a year on each student. That almost doubles the national average. Kids here are used to making the grade. Eight out of 10 will go to college, I mean the best colleges, because success is measured by a very high standard in Greenwich.

Note

Connecticut

    Connecticut is a small US state located in the northeastern United States of America. It has many industries but also large forests. The capital city is Hartford, which is the center for US insurance companies. Yale University is located in this state.

Part E Fun Time

Listening Script

Directions: Listen to a song entitled *Red Sails in the Sunset*. Most of the words in the *lyrics*（歌词）are provided below. Try to supply the missing words in the blanks.

Red Sails in the Sunset

Red sails in the sunset, way out on the sea
Oh, carry my loved one home safely to me
She sailed at the dawning, all day I've been blue
Red sails in the sunset, I'm trusting in you

Swift wings you must borrow
Make straight for the shore
We marry tomorrow
And she goes sailing no more

Red sails in the sunset, way out on the sea
Oh, carry my loved one home safely to me

Red sails in the sunset, way out on the sea
Oh, carry my loved one home safely to me

Key

1. in the sunset   2. at the dawning   3. Swift wings   4. tomorrow   5. way out on the sea   6. Red sails in the sunset

Notes

1. ***Red Sails in the Sunset***

   The song was written about Portstewart, a seaside town in County Londonderry, Northern Ireland. It was inspired by a beautiful summer evening in Portstewart. After songwriter Jimmy Kennedy（1902—1984）wrote the lyrics, Hugh Williams ［*pseudonym*（笔名）for Wilhelm Grosz （1894—1939）］wrote the music.

   The song became very popular soon and Portstewart today has an annual Red Sails Festival each July.

2. **way out on the sea**

   The word "way" is used as an adverb meaning "very far".

3. Swift wings you must borrow

   Make straight for the shore

   Here the songwriter used his imagination and hoped that the boat would have a pair of wings and fly directly back to shore.

54
大学英语自主听力指南 4

Historical Events

Preview

This unit integrates various useful expressions and authentic talks about historical events.

Objectives

After studying this unit, the students are expected to:
1. know the basic words and expressions about history;
2. understand conversations and short talks about different ways to talk about historical events;
3. be able to make brief comments on historical events.

Part A Language Focus

Notes

1. **medieval history**

    It refers to the Middle Ages, the period in Western European history between about AD 1100 and 1500. The ideas and institutions of western civilization derive largely from the events of the Early Middle Ages and the rebirth of culture in the later years.

2. **natural history**

    Natural history generally refers to the study and description of plants, animals and natural objects, especially their origins, evolution, and interrelationships.

3. BC（Before Christ 公元前），AD（Anno Domini 公元）

BC means "Before Christ", i. e. before the birth of *Christ*（耶稣基督）. AD comes from Latin, meaning "in the year of the *Lord*（上帝）".

4. prehistory

Prehistory is the time before people invented writing.

5. Stone Age

The Stone Age was a time in prehistory when humans made and used stone tools. Early humans began using stones as simple tools about 2 million years ago. Humans used mainly stone tools until about 10,000 years ago.

6. Age of Enlightenment

It is a period in the eighteenth century when many writers and scientists believed that science and knowledge, not religion, could improve people's lives.

Part B Authentic Conversations

Purpose

This part aims to familiarize the students with authentic conversations that can be heard in our daily life about historical events.

Detailed Plan

1. Study the new words and expressions in *Word Bank*.
2. Do the required exercises.
3. Check the answers.
4. Listen to the conversations again. Pay special attention to the parts you didn't understand or misunderstood. You may refer to the script if necessary.

Short Conversations

Listening Script

Directions: You will hear 6 conversations between two speakers. Listen to them and answer the following questions by choosing the right options.

1. Man:　　Over the long term I wonder if Jackie Kennedy's value is going to hold up as much as some

of the people who really did change the course of history.

Woman: Whether it will or won't is debatable.

Question: What does the woman think of Kennedy?

2. Man: Do you think schools should be allowed to teach the *Bible* as a historical document?

   Woman: I am not very sure about this, but I think there are many other books that can be used to teach history.

   Question: What is the woman's opinion about teaching history in schools?

3. Man: Chinese Traditional Medicine is as old as Chinese culture itself. Here in Hong Kong, patients and doctors rely on remedies that date back thousands of years to treat everything.

   Woman: It's wonderful that it is being so popular. But as I say, with that growing popularity of TCM comes an impact on the animal species that are used.

   Question: What is the woman worried about?

4. Woman: Have you been to a lot of different historical sites?

   Man: Yeah. Last week we took a trip around to the Civil War, visiting battle grounds and things back in 1860s. We read Bruce Catton's book before we went, and so we were ready to look up the places we read about. It was really interesting.

   Question: Why did the man read Bruce Catton's book before his trip?

5. Man: I just got out of a PhD program in history.

   Woman: In history?

   Man: Yes, in history. I am very frustrated most of the time when I was there. My concern is that my professors were using history as a political tool. They were re-writing history as it ought to have been, not as it actually was.

   Question: Why was the man frustrated while studying for his PhD?

6. Woman: From slavery to the Civil War, how we interpret and recall history isn't always the way the events originally happened. Over the years, teachers, historians, and journalists shape and revise history through their own personal accounts.

   Man: That's right. Have you heard the phrase "History is written by the winners"? To understand history you have to know who's writing it, why, and how they went about it.

   Question: What can be inferred from the conversation?

Key

1. D   2. C   3. D   4. D   5. C   6. A

Notes

1. Jackie Kennedy

   Jackie Kennedy (1929—1994) was born Jacqueline Lee Bouvier. She married John F. Kennedy, 35th president of the United States, in 1953. She was noted for her style and *elegance*

（高雅）. After the *assassination*（暗杀）of John Kennedy in 1963, she married again five years later. Her second husband, Aristotle Onassis, was one of the wealthiest men in the world.

2. Bible

The *Bible* is an important book to both *Jews*（犹太人）and *Christians*（基督教徒）. Its writings unite followers within each faith by giving them a common source for religious belief and practice. Although they include some of the same writings, the *Bible* of Judaism is different from the *Bible* of Christianity.

The *Bible* of the Christian religion consists of the Old *Testament*（旧约）and the New Testament.

3. The Civil War

It refers to the American Civil War. It was a military conflict between the United States of America（the Union）and the Confederate States of America（the Confederacy）from 1861 to 1865.

4. Bruce Catton

Bruce Catton（1899—1978）was an American historian, journalist, and editor who wrote extensively on the Civil War and edited（1954—1959）*American Heritage* magazine.

Longer Conversations

Conversation One

Listening Script

Directions: You will hear a conversation between two speakers. Listen to the conversation twice and answer the questions by choosing the right options.

Man: There are a lot of young people who do not like history. I mean they're the same way I was about math.

Woman: That's right. There are an awful lot of young people who don't like history. Because they think of history as textbook learning, memorizing names and dates.

Man: That's not what history is at all. History is conducting research. It's being a detective, getting into a museum or interviewing a member of the community who participated in a historical event. So it's conducting the research. If they are drawing meaning and then presenting these findings in these very creative and exciting formats, they will find history is actually fun.

Questions:

1. What does the man like?
2. Which of the following is not true of some young people's view on history?
3. What does the man think of history?

Key

1. B 2. C 3. A

Conversation Two

Listening Script

Directions: You will hear a conversation between two speakers. Listen to the conversation twice and write your answers to the questions in the space provided below.

Woman: I am really interested in how people learn about history. I have one concern that I was wondering if you would like to comment on. That is the current role of the media as it affects people's understanding of history, especially because a lot of history has been written in books, and more and more people now get their information through the media, and historians don't have the money to make movies to compete with the media.

Man: Well, I happen to be a great fan of the historical accounts. They're not always accurate — sometimes they are extremely inaccurate. But they present the history so vividly that they enable me as a teacher to build upon the memories. And my students like historical movies, because they get a portrayal, whether it's assassination of Kennedy or the more recent Liberty Series on the American Revolution. They have a very vivid sense of one interpretation of this event. I don't see it as a competitor at all. I see that the historical movies are very helpful in the teaching of history.

Questions:

1. What is the woman's concern?
2. What is the woman's opinion about the information given through the media?
3. What does the man think of historical movies?
4. Why do the man's students like historical movies?

Key

1. The influence of the media on people's understanding of history.
2. It may be misleading.
3. They are not always accurate, but they are very helpful in the teaching of history.
4. Because they get a portrayal and can have a very vivid sense of one interpretation of a certain event in history.

Notes

1. Kennedy

Kennedy (1917—1963), also known as Jack Kennedy and JFK, was President of the US from 1961 to 1963. He was an extremely popular president, and he planned to improve education, the system of medical care, and civil rights in the US. In 1963, he was shot in Dallas, Texas.

Part C   Talks from TV Programs

Purpose

This part consists of exercises based on talks excerpted from TV programs. The students are expected to understand such talks and get the necessary information from them.

Detailed Plan

1. Study the new words and expressions in *Word Bank*.
2. Do the exercises based on *Excerpt One* and *Excerpt Two*.
3. Check the answers.
4. Listen to the short talks again. Pay special attention to the parts you didn't understand or misunderstood. You may refer to the script if necessary.

Excerpt One

Listening Script

Directions：You will hear a short talk from a TV program. Listen to it twice and decide whether the following statements are true (T) or false (F) according to the short talk.

Ben Kingsley, Narrator：

In the 11th century，China's inventiveness surpasses all others. At that time，roads from the West to China crossed the terrible Takla Makan Desert. Its name meant "he who enters will never

大学英语自主听力指南 4

return."

The gateway to China was Dunhuang. Here, each of the 450 caves was a shrine decorated by monks. On the ceilings and walls, they painted the world of China. It was a land of mountains and cities, singers and devils.

The Chinese regarded their land as the central country of the world. They believed their emperor held a mandate from heaven to rule all the peoples of the Earth.

China's vast distances were conquered by technology. The Grand Canal linked its five great rivers into one waterway 1,500 miles long. It led to the capital of Chinese emperors. In the 11th century, the city of Kaifeng. To feed its million people, the markets were open 24 hours a day.

Most remarkable of all, the people of Kaifeng already used inventions most of the rest of the world still waited for. They had printing, paper money, the compass, an earthquake detector, a clock driven by water, acupuncture and gunpowder.

The Chinese had kites which carried people. They used them to pioneer their dreams of flight. They used them to make music and to measure distances. Even the emperor designed kites. This vast empire was schooled and united by the ancient philosophy of one man, Confucius.

Key

1. T   2. F   3. F   4. T   5. T   6. T   7. F   8. T

Notes

1. Ben Kingsley

Ben Kingsley (1943—   ) is a British actor. He won the Oscar award for his performance as Indian leader Mohandas Gandhi in the 1982 film *Gandhi*. He is also the narrator of CNN's TV series *Millennium* (千周年纪念).

2. the terrible Takla Makan Desert

The Takla Makan Desert (塔克拉玛干沙漠) is in the *Xinjiang Uigur Autonomous Region* (新疆维吾尔自治区) of China. It is known as one of the largest sandy deserts in the world. The ancient trade route between China and the West is known as the Silk Road. It basically followed the Great Wall of China to the northwest, bypassed the Takla Makan Desert, climbed the *Pamir* (帕米尔) Mountains, crossed *Afghanistan* (阿富汗), and continued west through the modern-day countries of Iran, Iraq, Syria, and Turkey.

3. Dunhuang

Dunhuang is a city in Jiuquan, Gansu province, China. In ancient times, it was the center of trade between China and its western neighbors. Today, this historical city attracts a lot of tourists because of the Mogao Caves.

4. the Grand Canal

This is an inland waterway, about 1,609 km (1,000 *mi*) long, of eastern China extending from Tianjin in the north to Hangzhou in the south.

5. Kaifeng

Kaifeng is a city situated in northern China, in the Huang He valley of northern Henan Province. It was the capital of the northern Song Dynasty (960—1127).

Excerpt Two

Listening Script

Directions: You will hear a short talk from a TV program. Listen to it twice and write your answers to the questions in the space provided below.

The explorers have left monuments all over the world.

One of the most meaningful, and at the same time little-known, is to be found high on a hilltop in Nova Scotia.

Here, alone with the sigh of the wind, are the graves of Alexander Graham Bell and his wife, Mabel.

Bell called their estate here Beinn Bhreagh, or "beautiful mountain."

In the late 1800s Bell spent much of his time promoting the National Geographic Society.

It was a favorite preoccupation of a man whose boundless creativity changed everyone's life forever.

Inventing the telephone made Bell's fortune.

It also freed him to pursue his many interests and enjoy his growing family.

Enthusiastic, generous, and warmhearted, Bell became a grandfather figure to the world.

When young Gilbert Hovey Grosvenor caught the eye of Bell's elder daughter, Elsie, Bell offered him a job in Washington. The couple was married in 1900. They set up housekeeping not far from Grosvenor's office at 15th Street and Pennsylvania Avenue.

It was an exciting time to be alive. Americans were thrilled by modern innovations and their growing political power.

Grosvenor became the first full-time employee of *National Geographic*, which was kept going mainly by Bell's contributions.

In a tiny office sometimes piled high with unsold magazines, Grosvenor worked to realize Bell's hope that Geographic's journal could somehow pay the Society's way.

Questions:

1. What can be found on a hilltop in Nova Scotia?
2. What did Bell do with his boundless creativity?
3. Retell some of the words that are used in praise of Bell.
4. Why did Bell offer Grosvenor a job?
5. How did Americans feel during the time of great innovations?
6. How did Grosvenor manage to keep the magazine *National Geographic* going?
7. What did Bell hope that *National Geographic* could do?

Key

1. Graves of Alexander Graham Bell and his wife, Mabel.
2. He changed everyone's life forever.
3. Enthusiastic, generous, and warmhearted, Bell became a grandfather figure to the world.
4. He caught the eye of Bell's elder daughter, Elsie.
5. Americans were thrilled by modern innovations and their growing political power.
6. He got contributions from Bell.
7. He hoped that the magazine could finally support the National Geographic Society.

Notes

1. Nova Scotia

Nova Scotia is one of Canada's *maritime*（邻海的）provinces. No part of Nova Scotia is more than 56 kilometers from the sea, which is key to life in the province.

2. Alexander Graham Bell and his wife, Mabel

The famous inventor Alexander Graham Bell（1847—1922）invented the telephone in 1876. In 1877, Bell established the Bell Telephone Company. Later that year, he married Mabel Hubbard, For many years Bell spent his summers at his estate in Nova Scotia. He died there on Aug. 2, 1922. During the funeral service every telephone of the Bell system in the United States and Canada was kept silent.

3. Beinn Bhreagh

As a Scottish-born American, Bell called his estate in Nova Scotia "Beinn Bhreagh", which means "beautiful mountain" in Scottish *Gaelic*（盖尔语）.

4. National Geographic Society

National Geographic Society is an organization in the US that is known for its magazines and television shows about nature, animals, and people from cultures all over the world. It was founded in 1888 in Washington, D. C. of the United States.

5. Gilbert Hovey Grosvenor

Grosvenor, Gilbert Hovey（1875—1966）was born in Istanbul, Turkey, on Oct. 28, 1875. He edited National Geographic Magazine for more than 50 years. During this time, he helped create popular interest in geography and exploration by presenting lively articles on people, wildlife, and natural wonders in the world.

6. Elsie

Elsie May Bell（1878—1964）was Alexander Bell's eldest daughter.

7. Pennsylvania Avenue

Pennsylvania Avenue is a street in Washington, D. C. of the US, joining *the White House* （白宫）and *the United States Capitol*（国会大厦）.

8. *National Geographic*

This is a monthly magazine of geography, archaeology and exploration published in Washington, D. C. of the US. It is especially well known for its beautiful photographs. The magazine was founded in 1888 and still is published by the National Geographic Society.

Part D Dictation

Purpose

This part contains a short talk to be dictated to the students. This exercise trains the students' skills in

writing down what they have heard.

Detailed Plan

1. Study the new words and expressions in *Word Bank*.
2. Listen to the short talk from the beginning to the end without any pause.
3. Write down the sentences during the pauses when the short talk is spoken again.
4. Read the listening script and correct whatever mistakes the students may have made.
5. Listen to the short talk again if necessary.

Listening Script

Directions: You will hear a short talk about the Industrial Revolution. The short talk will be spoken twice. After you listen to it at normal speed, the short talk will be spoken again with pauses. During the pauses, write down what you hear in the space provided below.

The Industrial Revolution began in Britain in about 1750 and within 100 years the country developed from an agricultural society into an industrial nation with trading links across the world. Industry has a great effect on British social and economic life, as many people moved from the countryside to work in the rapidly growing towns.

In the US the Industrial Revolution brought similar changes. In 1790 only 5% of Americans lived in cities but by 1940 more than half had moved to urban areas. Starting a factory required a lot of money and a new class of rich people, called capitalists, began to appear.

Note

Industrial Revolution

The Industrial Revolution was a period in the late 18th and early 19th centuries when great changes took place in the way farming was practiced and the way products were made. The Industrial Revolution began in England and spread to all parts of the world.

Part E   Fun Time

Directions: Listen to a humorous story about a tour guide and a group of tourists. Tell what time it is when the man says "Just missed it by a half hour!"

A bus load of tourists arrives at Runnymede. They gather around the guide who says, "This is the spot where the barons forced King John to sign the *Magna Carta*."

A fellow at the front of the crowd asks, "When did that happen?"

"1215," answers the guide.

The man looks at his watch and says, "Damn! Just missed it by a half hour!"

Notes

1. **Runnymede**

   Runnymede is a field beside the River Thames in southern England. At this site in June 1215, the barons of England forced King John to approve *Magna Carta*, a document that limited the powers of the king.

2. **King John**

   John Plantagenet (1167—1216) was king of England from 1199 to 1216. The Magna Carta was issued during his reign. King John has been called the worst king ever to rule England.

3. **Magna Carta**

   This is an important historical document that King John was forced to sign in 1215. It gave some political and legal rights to the English people.

4. **1215**

   This refers to the year when *Magna Carta* was signed. In the story, the man thought the tour guide was talking about the time. He must be looking at his watch which shows 12:45. That's why he says "Just missed it by a half hour".

Unit 7

Automobiles

Preview

This unit integrates various useful expressions and authentic talks about automobiles.

Objectives

After studying this unit, the students are expected to:
1. know the basic words and expressions about automobiles;
2. understand conversations and short talks about automobiles;
3. be able to make brief comments on automobiles.

Part A Language Focus

Notes

1. **Speed limits in different countries**
   The following table shows the default speed limits that apply in various countries.

Country	Within Towns	Automobiles & Motorcycles		Trucks or Automobiles with Trailer	
		Outside Built-up Areas/Expressways	Motorways	Outside Built-up Areas/Expressways	Motorways
Australia	50	100~130 (Previously Unlimited)	100~110	90~100	90~100

(**To be continued**)

Country	Within Towns	Automobiles & Motorcycles		Trucks or Automobiles with Trailer	
		Outside Built-up Areas/Expressways	Motorways	Outside Built-up Areas/Expressways	Motorways
Canada	40~60	70~110	100~110	80~100	100~110
China	40~60	60~80	100~120	N/A	N/A
France	50	90~110	130	90~110	130
Germany	50	100	no speed limit	60(trucks)~80	80~100
India	50	100	80	65	40
Japan	40~60	50~60	60~100	50~60	80
Korea, South	30~80	60~80	80~120	40~60	80
Russia	60	90~110	110	70~90	90
Singapore	50	80~90	90	60	60
United Kingdom	48 (30 mph)	97~113 (60~70 mph)	113 (70 mph)	64~97 (40~60 mph)	97 (60 mph)
United States	24~72 (15~45 mph)	89~121 (55~75 mph)	89~129 (55~80 mph)	Restrictions only in some states, typically 5~15 mph lower.	

2. parking meter

   A parking meter is a device used to collect money in exchange for the right to park a vehicle in a particular place for a limited amount of time.

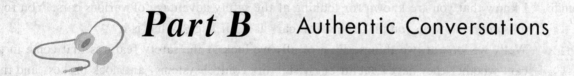

Part B   Authentic Conversations

Purpose

This part aims to familiarize the students with authentic conversations that can be heard in our daily life about automobiles.

Detailed Plan

1. Study the new words and expressions in *Word Bank*.
2. Do the required exercises.
3. Check the answers.
4. Listen to the conversations again. Pay special attention to the parts you didn't understand or misunderstood. You may refer to the script if necessary.

Short Conversations

Listening Script

Directions: You will hear 6 conversations between two speakers. Listen to them and answer the following questions by choosing the right options.

1. Man: Ellen, what kind of car do you think you're going to buy?
   Woman: Well, I've been thinking about buying a van, because it'd be nice to pack the kids and the dog in.
   Man: Are you going to buy a minivan or buy a full size?
   Woman: I don't know. But definitely the next car I'll get will be a used car because I can't afford a new one. It is so expensive.
   Question: What kind of car will the woman buy?

2. Woman: Well, how do you like your Volvo?
   Man: Um, it is fine. I had like a hundred and twenty thousand miles on it and only had to change the oil. I never have a problem with it, but it is an old one.
   Woman: Are you going to sell it?
   Man: I wouldn't trade it for anything.
   Question: What is the man going to do with his Volvo?

3. Woman: I know that you are known for looking at the safety advantage of various cars. You focus on safety. How do you pick the safest car? Is it air bags? What is it?
   Man: Well, we look at two things. First of all, we look at the safety features that come in the car, whether they have dual air bags, stability control systems, anti-lock brakes, and then we look at the front and side crash tests.
   Question: How does the man know if a car is safe or not?

4. Man: Yeah, one of the other issues you look at is maintenance. Issues like warranties.
   Woman: Right. Warranties are critically important, because that's the best way you can save money on buying a car.
   Man: You know, it seems like the warranty always runs out and then your car breaks down the

next day.

Question: What does the man mean?

5. Man: Good morning, can I help you?

Woman: Yes, and, you know, I have finished college and am going into the market. I need a car, but really can't afford it now until I get established and get some money saved. I am looking for a $2,000~$3,000 car.

Man: Well, what can you buy in today's market for $2,000 or $3,000? A car like this has a lot of potential problems. It could cost you a lot more in the long run keeping it going. I think leasing a used car is a good choice.

Question: What is the most probable relationship between the speakers?

6. Man: This is the Audi AL2 and it's made primarily of aluminum. Aluminum makes the car lighter, makes it more gas-efficient. This is a car that Audi intends as a family-friendly car.

Woman: And this is a — and this is a prototype, Christopher?

Man: Yes, this is a prototype. It'll be available in Europe very soon this year.

Question: Which of the following is not true about Audi AL2?

Key

1. B　2. C　3. A　4. C　5. D　6. D

Notes

1. van

A van is a kind of vehicle used for transporting goods or groups of people. It has different types. In the United States a full-size van is usually a large, boxy vehicle.

Minivans are usually much smaller in size. Minivans offer similar seating capacity (traditionally seven passengers), and better fuel economy than full-size vans.

2. Volvo

The Volvo Group is a Swedish supplier of commercial vehicles such as trucks, buses and construction equipment, etc. Over the years Volvo has earned a reputation for its attentiveness to quality control and safety features.

3. anti-lock brakes

Anti-lock braking systems, commonly known as ABS, are used to control *skidding*(溜滑,侧滑) on roads during hard braking.

4. front and side crash tests

There are a number of well-known crash test programs around the world, including NCAP (New Car Assessment Program, US), EuroNCAP (Europe), ANCAP (Australia) and JapNCAP (Japan).

Frontal-impact tests are usually impacts upon a solid concrete wall at a specified speed. In a side-impact test, an *impactor*(碰撞体) representing the front of a car is used to strike the sides of the vehicles being assessed.

Longer Conversations

Conversation One

Listening Script

Directions: You will hear a conversation between two speakers. Listen to the conversation twice and answer the questions by choosing the right options.

Man: One of the most annoying sounds in the city — especially at midnight when you're trying to sleep — is the siren of a car alarm.

Woman: You are right. If you try to get a decent night's sleep, invariably you're going to be awakened by the shrieking of car alarms.

Man: As a matter of fact, I don't think car alarms do much good to car safety. Most people just ignore them and never answer them. And thieves have learned to defeat them.

Woman: I know. But the companies that sell car alarms insist these devices do prevent car theft, and they say their newest products are more sophisticated and more effective than ever.

Man: Have you bought a car alarm for your Honda Civic?

Woman: Yes, it costs me a couple of hundred dollars which is a small price to pay to protect a car.

Questions:

1. What are the speakers talking about?
2. Which of the following is not true according to the man?
3. What do the companies say about their newest car alarms?
4. Why does the woman buy a car alarm?

Key

1. C 2. C 3. B 4. D

Note

Honda Civic

The Honda Civic is a *compact*（紧凑型的）car manufactured by *Honda*（本田）, a Japanese maker of motorcycles and cars. The company started as a motorbike maker in 1949, but by the 1980s, it was already a multinational corporation with plants in about 30 countries.

Conversation Two

Listening Script

Directions: You will hear a conversation between two speakers. Listen to the conversation twice and decide whether the following statements are true (T) or false (F) according to the conversation.

Woman: The assembly line is great if you're going to produce massive numbers of absolutely standardized part or products. Once the consumer wants something different, the assembly line is an immensely complicated and costly operation to shift.

Man: You are right. It's the reason why you can't have a car built to your personal tastes. You have to choose one of the standard varieties that the factory turns out. And the other problem is that most of the people Henry Ford hired to work in his factory, hated it; hated the machine-driven pace of work.

Woman: Really?

Man: Yes. That's one reason why, even today, up to a quarter of the work at big American car assembly plants is just fixing mistakes, repairing cars that come off the assembly line with defects. But Toyota and Honda have figured out how to make the assembly line respond more quickly to consumer demand, and how to turn out cars that are pretty nearly perfect.

Key

1. F   2. T   3. F   4. T   5. F

Notes

1. assembly line

An assembly line is a manufacturing system for making things in a factory in which each worker deals with only one part of a product. It is used to assemble quickly large numbers of a uniform product. The best-known form of the assembly line was realized into practice by Ford Motor Company between 1908 and 1915. Traditional assembly lines had come under criticism from those concerned with their effects on workers, but industrial *robots*（机器人）now perform many of the repetitive tasks.

2. Henry Ford

Henry Ford（1863—1947）was the American founder of the Ford Motor Company and father of modern assembly lines used in mass production. His introduction of the Model T automobile revolutionized transportation and American industry. As owner of the Ford Company he became one of the richest and best-known people in the world. Ford left most of his vast wealth to the Ford Foundation but arranged for his family to control the company permanently.

3. Toyota

Toyota（丰田）is one of the largest automobile manufacturers in the world.

The current corporation began in the 1930s. Today it has assembly plants and distributors in many foreign countries, and its vehicles, some in the form of unassembled units, are exported to more than 140 countries.

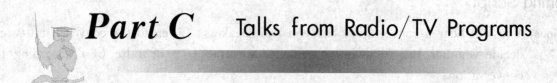

Part C   Talks from Radio/TV Programs

Purpose

This part consists of exercises based on talks excerpted from radio/TV programs. The students are expected to understand such talks and get the necessary information from them.

Detailed Plan

1. Study the new words and expressions in *Word Bank*.
2. Do the exercises based on *Excerpt One* and *Excerpt Two*.
3. Check the answers.
4. Listen to the short talks again. Pay special attention to the parts you didn't understand or misunderstood. You may refer to the script if necessary.

Excerpt One

Listening Script

Directions: You will hear a short talk from a radio program. Listen to it twice and write your answers to the questions in the space provided below.

Neal Conan, host: One hundred years ago next month, Charles and Frank Duryea drove the first car down the streets of Springfield. Jim Wren was not there to see it himself but he is among the nation's leading authorities on automotive history. Mr. Wren has just retired as director of patents for the American Automobile Manufacturers Association and he joins us from his home in Detroit. Good morning.

Jim Wren: Good morning.

Conan: Tell us about that first car.

Wren: Well, that first car was actually driven by J. Frank Duryea, Charles happened to be out of town at the time and although it didn't operate that well in the first drive, some three years later, Charles and Frank established the Duryea Motor Wagon

Conan: Company and produced 13 cars, which started the American automobile industry.

Conan: What were some of the terrifying speeds this car would reach?

Wren: Oh, boy, you're looking at speeds — the speed limits in those early days were only 8 to 12 miles an hour although there were great expectations for the automobile in most American cities, mainly because of the congestion with the horses and the wagons and so on. When it came, it created such chaos they immediately put restrictive speed limits on it.

Conan: And, of course, it had to share the road with all those horses.

Wren: Yes and it was utter chaos. In fact, it was so bad that Uriah Smith of Battle Creek, Michigan, came up with the idea of fashioning an automobile with the front of it looking like a horse's head. That shows you the kind of problem they had in those early days.

Questions:

1. Why is Mr. Wren invited to talk on the radio program?
2. Where does Mr. Wren have a talk with the host?
3. Who drove the first car?
4. What kind of company did Charles and Frank establish?
5. What were the speed limits in those early days?
6. Why did people put restrictive speed limits on the car?
7. Why did Uriah Smith design a car with the front of it looking like a horse's head?

Key

1. Because he is one of the nation's leading authorities on automotive history.
2. He has a talk with the host from his home in Detroit.
3. Frank.
4. They established a motor wagon company.
5. The speed limits in those early days were 8 to 12 miles an hour.
6. Because the streets were crowded with horses and wagons.
7. Because there was a confrontation between an automobile and a horse.

Notes

1. **Charles and Frank Duryea**

   Charles Edgar Duryea (1861—1938) and James Frank Duryea (1869—1967) were brothers who built one of the first American automobiles (1893).

2. **Detroit**

   Detroit is the largest city in Michigan of the US and one of the world's greatest industrial centers. More automobiles are produced in the Detroit area than anywhere else in the United States. Detroit is often called the Automobile Capital of the World or Motor City. Detroit is also a chief US port and transportation center.

3. **American Automobile Manufacturers Association**

   The American Automobile Manufacturers Association (AAMA) was a trade association comprised of Chrysler Corporation, Ford Motor Company, and General Motors Corporation, the three traditional US-based manufacturers of passenger cars and light trucks.

In January 1999, AAMA was replaced by The Alliance of Automobile Manufacturers because the former had represented only American manufacturers.

4. Duryea Motor Wagon Company

The Duryea Motor Wagon Company, established in 1895 by the Duryea brothers, was the first American firm to build gasoline automobiles.

5. Uriah Smith

Since horses were quite frightened of cars, they were a great worry for the first drivers. Uriah Smith, the founder of the Horsey Horseless Carriage Company in Battle Creek, Michigan had a solution. His motor car came with a wooden, life-sized horse head on the front.

Excerpt Two

Listening Script

Directions: You will hear a short talk from a TV program. Listen to it twice and answer the questions by choosing the right options.

Greg Hunter, CNN Correspondent:

(voice-over) The 2001 Ford F-150 pickup was one of the worst performers in the Insurance Institute for Highway Safety crash test. Look at the way the cab folds on impact. Compare that to the redesigned 2004 model where the cab stays intact.

Anne McCartt, Insurance Institute for Highway Safety: When we looked at driver death rates, what we saw was the newer F-150 had a death rate half that of the older model.

Hunter (on camera): What an improvement!

McCartt: It's a dramatic improvement. This is a much safer vehicle now.

Hunter (voice-over): The institute compiles statistics on driver death rates for more than 200 vehicles, between the years 2001 and 2004, the latest data available, ranking the best and the worst, according to class and size.

Smaller cars had generally higher death rates, but some cars did much better than others in that category. The Mini Cooper had one third of the fatalities of the Acura RSX.

(on camera.) Does it have something to do with quality?

McCartt: Quality is definitely an important factor.

Hunter (voice-over): Large, heavy vehicles tend to have the lowest death rates. And SUVs, which have a tendency to roll over, are getting safer, mainly because of electronic stability control.

(on camera) Aren't some of these vehicles that have low death rates just built better?

McCartt: They are built better. They're ... They're built — and what I mean by "built better" is they're built so that they do a very good job protecting occupants in the event of a crash.

Hunter: A Honda spokesman told CNN the lower rated Acura RSX tends to appeal to younger, less experienced drivers.

Questions:

1. What do you know about the 2004 Ford F-150 pickup from the conversation?
2. How many vehicles were compared in terms of safety by the Insurance Institute for Highway Safety?
3. Compared with the Acura RSX, what was the death rate for the Mini Cooper?
4. Why are SUVs getting safer?
5. What does the Honda spokesman mean at the end of the talk?

Key

1. A 2. B 3. B 4. D 5. C

Notes

1. **Ford F-150 pickup**

    The F-Series is a series of pickup trucks made by Ford Motor Company. It has been sold for over 5 decades. The F-150 has been the best-selling vehicle in the United States for over 2 decades and the best-selling truck for 30 years.

2. **the Insurance Institute for Highway Safety**

    The Insurance Institute for Highway Safety is a US non-profit organization funded by auto insurers. It works to reduce the number of motor vehicle crashes.

3. **Anne McCartt**

    Anne T. McCartt, Ph.D., is Senior Vice President, Research, at the Insurance Institute for Highway Safety.

4. **Mini Cooper**

    Born in Kingston, Surrey, England, John Newton Cooper (1923—2000) was a co-founder, with his father Charles Cooper, of the Cooper Car Company.

    The Mini Cooper was first introduced in 1961. Because it was affordable, stylish, fun to drive and easy to park anywhere, the Mini Cooper quickly achieved great success around the world.

5. **Acura RSX**

    The Acura RSX was an automobile sold by Honda in North America and Hong Kong.

6. **electronic stability control**

    Electronic Stability Control (or ESC) is a crash avoidance system found on many vehicles. Unlike air bags, which only help the driver and passengers during a collision, ESC will help to avoid loss of control that could lead to a collision.

Part D Dictation

Purpose

This part contains a short talk to be dictated to the learners. This exercise trains the students' skills in

writing down what they have heard.

Detailed Plan

1. Study the new words and expressions in *Word Bank*.
2. Listen to the short talk from the beginning to the end without any pause.
3. Write down the sentences during the pauses when the short talk is spoken again.
4. Read the listening script and correct whatever mistakes the students may have made.
5. Listen to the short talk again if necessary.

Listening Script

Directions: You will hear a short talk about automobiles. The short talk will be spoken twice. After you listen to it at normal speed, the short talk will be spoken again with pauses. During the pauses, write down what you hear in the space provided below.

The first production of cars started coming off assembly lines just over 100 years ago. And since then, they have changed the world. We could easily look back at the 20th century and describe it as the age of the automobile.

The automobile changed the economics of real estate. Land that had been too far away from cities to be valuable soon became high-priced because the automobile made these places accessible.

The automobile also brought us the motel, fast-food restaurants, the drive-up shopping mall, and the drive-up bank. As a matter of fact, it brought us the drive-up everything.

Note

drive-up+n.

It means a place in a commercial establishment such as a restaurant or bank where customers are served while remaining in their cars. For example, a drive-up bank, a drive-up restaurant.

Part E Fun Time

Listening Script

Directions: Listen to a humorous story about two drivers who have had a traffic accident. Tell what the policeman will do when he arrives.

Two men got out of their cars after they collided at an intersection. One took a bottle from his pocket and said to the other, "Here, maybe you'd like a nip to calm your nerves." "Thanks," he said, and took a long pull from the bottle. "Here, you have one, too," he added, handing back the whiskey.

"Well, I'd rather not," said the first. "At least not until after the police have been here."

Note

At least not until after the police have been here.

As in any place of the world, drunk driving is strictly prohibited. In the story, the driver who takes a drink of whiskey will be in trouble when the policeman arrives because the policeman will take for granted that he has caused the accident as a result of drunk driving.

Aging

Preview

This unit integrates various useful expressions and authentic talks about aging.

Objectives

After studying this unit, the students are expected to:

1. know the basic words and expressions about age and aging;
2. understand conversations and short talks about age and aging;
3. be able to make brief comments on problems related to old age and aging using the words and expressions learnt in this unit.

Part A Language Focus

Notes

1. **aging**

   Aging is the process of growing old. In most human beings, the changes do not become visible until individuals reach 30 to 40 years of age. Age-related changes include graying or loss of hair, weakened muscles, wrinkled skin, and diminished sense of hearing and vision.

2. **old age**

   It is difficult to define old age because its meaning varies in different societies. People may be considered old because of certain changes in their activities or social roles. For example, people may be considered old when they become grandparents or when they begin to do less or different work. In the United States, many people think of 65 as the beginning of old age because that's the age for retirement. In China, most men retire at 60 and women at 55.

Part B   Authentic Conversations

Purpose

This part aims to familiarize the students with authentic conversations that can be heard in our daily life about aging.

Detailed Plan

1. Study the new words and expressions in *Word Bank*.
2. Do the required exercises.
3. Check the answers.
4. Listen to the conversations again. Pay special attention to the parts you didn't understand or misunderstood. You may refer to the script if necessary.

Short Conversations

Listening Script

Directions: You will hear 6 conversations between two speakers. Listen to them and answer the following questions by choosing the right options.

1. Woman: How quickly the world is aging!
   Man: Yes, average life expectancy in 1900 was just 30. Now it is more than 60. Today, the average age in the world is 27. By 2025 it will be 32. By 2050, it will be 36. That means there will be more and more elderly people.
   Question: What will the average age in the world be by the year 2025?

2. Man: What do you think are some of the economic impacts of global aging?
   Woman: It has always been assumed that the market keeps growing. But in Europe decreasing demand leads to a decreasing market. People take less risk with investments. They are less mobile, so that affects the tourism industries. There are fewer consumers, because

older people already bought the major things they need.

Questions: Which of the following is not considered as one of the economic impacts of global aging?

3. Man: Old age is sounding better all the time. Is there a downside to all this joy?

   Woman: Unfortunately, yes. Older people are more likely to focus on the positive when making decisions. That can be dangerous, especially when it comes to finances.

   Questions: What does the woman think of older people?

4. Man: What is your opinion on the severe calorie-restricted diet being promoted by some people to slow the aging process?

   Woman: We don't have the evidence yet that significant calorie restriction in humans will extend life or slow aging, but the studies in animals are quite compelling.

   Question: What can we learn from the conversation?

5. Woman: It seems that the elderly are more likely to be women than men, especially in the top age groups.

   Man: Yes, most are widows and many live alone, often far from their families. So friendships among older women provide them an informal but important social network, helping them to live on their own and keeping them from having to move in with relatives or into a retirement home.

   Question: Who can help older women to live on their own according to the conversation?

6. Woman: You're 80. Has your view on aging changed as you've aged?

   Man: No, actually it has not changed much as I have grown older, but I am aware even more of the reality of age discrimination, and also of the preciousness of life and especially the great importance of family. I am a father of four wonderful daughters who remain loyal in both practical and loving ways.

   Question: Which of the following is not mentioned among the things that have drawn the man's attention more than before?

Key

1. C   2. A   3. C   4. B   5. C   6. D

Notes

1. **life expectancy**

   Life expectancy is a statistical measure of the average number of years that a group of people of a certain age may expect to live. This measure is based on the death rates by age for a specific population at a specific time.

2. **retirement home**

   Retirement home is a housing facility intended for the elderly. The usual pattern is that each person or couple in the home has an apartment-style room. Additional facilities are provided within the building, including facilities for meals, gathering, recreation, and some form of health care. A retirement home differs from a nursing home primarily in the level of medical care given.

Longer Conversations

Conversation One

Listening Script

Directions: You will hear a conversation between two speakers. Listen to the conversation twice and answer the questions by choosing the right options.

Woman: How do you feel about sending an elderly family member to a nursing home?

Man: Well, of course it's one of the last few things in the world you'd ever want to do unless it's really for their own good.

Woman: Oh, yes. I'd be very, very careful to place my mother in a nursing home. She had a rather massive stroke about eight months ago. Actually my mother-in-law was also confined to a nursing home for a while two years ago. She had a fall and could not take care of the house. That was really not a very good experience. Fortunately she only had to stay a few weeks and was able to return to her apartment again.

Man: That sounds good. Probably the hardest thing in my family was my grandmother had to be put in a nursing home. She had Parkinson's Disease and it got so much that she could not take care of herself anymore. That was not only a change of location. It was also very disturbing for her because she had been so used to traveling. She had children all across the United States and, you know, she spent nine months out of the year just visiting her children.

Woman: Probably she cannot travel for the rest of her life.

Man: Right. But the toughest for her, I think, is when she finally came to the realization that "I cannot take care of myself."

Woman: Oh, I can imagine that's really tough.

Questions:

1. What will the man do on the issue of taking care of an elderly member in his family?
2. What happened to the woman's mother?
3. Who was able to go back home again after a short stay in the nursing home?
4. What is the toughest for the man's grandmother?

Key

1. C 2. B 3. D 4. C

Notes

1. nursing home

  Nursing home is a residential institution that provides medical or nonmedical care, chiefly for people who are 65 years old or older. Nearly all homes also accept younger patients and try to provide a comfortable, homelike environment for their residents.

2. Parkinson's Disease

Parkinson's disease is a disorder of the brain that reduces muscle control. Most cases affect people from 50 to 70 years old. The disease is named for the English physician James Parkinson, who in 1817 first described it. Symptoms include trembling hands, rigid muscles, slow movement, and balance difficulties. The cause of Parkinson's disease is still unknown.

Conversation Two

Listening Script

Directions: You will hear a conversation between two speakers. Listen to the conversation twice and write your answers to the questions in the space provided below.

Man: Can you give me your views on the care of the elderly?

Woman: Well, I would hate to see them being put into a health care facility environment because they then feel like the family has abandoned them. I get the comments from elderly people that are still hanging on to their homes that their greatest fear is to be put into a care facility because the families then seem to neglect visiting them.

Man: I agree with you. In my grandfather's case, after he found out he was going to go into a nursing home, he passed away about a week after that.

Woman: He was sure afraid of being put in that kind of facility.

Man: Yes, we all felt very sorry. So after the death of my grandfather, we tried to keep my grandmother at home with us. Right now she is still able to walk around and do some things for herself. She gets Meals on Wheels which I think is a great thing because it saves people from having to prepare food for her.

Woman: And you don't have to worry about her leaving a stove on or whatever. It makes life a little bit easier.

Questions:

1. Why does the woman hate to see the elderly being put in a health care facility environment?
2. What is the greatest fear of elderly people who are still hanging on to their homes?
3. What happened to the man's grandfather one week after he found out he was going into a nursing home?
4. How is the man's grandmother now?
5. What would the man have to do without the service offered by Meals on Wheels?

Key

1. Because the elderly would feel like the family has abandoned them.
2. Their greatest fear is to be put into a care facility.

3. He passed away.
4. She is still able to walk around and do some things for herself.
5. He would have to prepare food for her.

Note

Meals on Wheels

   Meals on Wheels refers to programs that deliver meals to individuals at home who are unable to purchase or prepare their own meals. Because they are homebound, many of the recipients are the elderly.

Part C   Talks from Radio Programs

Purpose

This part consists of exercises based on talks excerpted from radio programs. The students are expected to understand such talks and get the necessary information from them.

Detailed Plan

1. Study the new words and expressions in *Word Bank*.
2. Do the exercises based on *Excerpt One* and *Excerpt Two*.
3. Check the answers.
4. Listen to the short talks again. Pay special attention to the parts you didn't understand or misunderstood. You may refer to the script if necessary.

Excerpt One

Listening Script

Directions: You will hear a short talk from a radio program. Listen to it twice and complete the following summary.

   Until recently, most scientists believed that aging was inevitable; that after a certain number of years, our bodies begin to show wear and tear, and we're afflicted with the diseases of aging: arthritis, heart disease, Alzheimer's. But now new findings may be rewriting that theory.

   Two independent teams of scientists from Germany and Japan reported last month, in the *Science* magazine，that they identified the gene that could stop our cells from aging. And another research team from the United States reported progress in understanding how worms with a certain gene mutation can live far longer than normal. This may possibly help us understand human aging，since these worms genetically seem to be pretty close to humans.

This hour we'll be talking about these latest findings in aging research，and what they mean for human aging; and how we may be at a point in history where aging may be understood，and，who knows? Controlled. Controlling aging，that's an exciting topic. Some really exciting research is going on.

If you'd like to talk about it，please. Our number is 1 – 800 – 989 – 8255. And if you'd like to get some interesting links on our website，please surf over to sciencefriday.com at www.sciencefriday.com，where you'll find links to this topic.

Key

Most scientists believed that aging was 1) <u>inevitable</u>. It seems that people are afflicted with 2) <u>diseases of aging</u>. But now new findings may be 3) <u>rewriting that theory</u>. Two teams of scientists reported that they identified the gene that could 4) <u>stop cells from aging</u>. Another team reported progress in understanding how worms with a certain gene mutation can 5) <u>live far longer than normal</u>. If you'd like to join us on the topic of aging，our number is 6) <u>1 – 800 – 989 – 8255</u>. If you'd like to find links to this topic，our website is 7) <u>www.sciencefriday.com</u>.

Notes

1. **Alzheimer's**

   Alzheimer's disease is a brain disease that causes increasing loss of memory and other mental abilities. The disease occurs in about 20 percent of people who live to age 85. The disease is named for the German psychiatrist Alois Alzheimer，who first described its effects on brain cells in 1907.

2. *Science* **magazine**

   Science is the academic journal of the American Association for the Advancement of Science and is considered one of the world's best scientific journals.

3. **gene mutation**

   This refers to a sudden and permanent change in a gene. When *DNA*（脱氧核糖核酸）is working correctly it keeps the body functioning properly and allows it to reproduce. Mutations of the DNA can cause diseases or other problems.

Excerpt Two

Listening Script

Directions：You will hear a short talk from a radio program. Listen to it twice and write your answers to the questions in the space provided below.

I believe in learning about growing old by meeting people who are already old.

Thirty years ago, visiting my grandmother, I met a man named Herb Feitler. He and I spent the better part of a day together, going to flea markets and into the desert communities around Palm Springs. I was in my early 20s, and driving around with this 80-year-old guy at the wheel of his enormous Oldsmobile seemed to me like the height of exotica. Later I realized what made the experience so novel: He was the first old person I'd spent time with who wasn't in my family.

In the late 1970's I worked at a small nursing home. Most of the residents were at least three times my age. Now, nearly 30 years later, I never encounter anyone even twice my age. But I continue to meet and befriend elderly people.

After my father suffered a stroke, he started going to an adult day center. Instead of being around people who viewed what had befallen him as tragic, he met a new group of people who didn't know him before. They understood that the way he was now — needing assistance when he walked, speaking softly — was not the way he had always been. But they simply accepted him as he was. This was liberating for him. Even though his range of movement was smaller and his voice far quieter than it had been, his health was bolstered by these new relationships.

As I grow old, I know issues that were once of great concern to me won't seem important anymore. I believe that having something new happen, no matter how small, is what makes for a healthy day, no matter how many days may be left.

Questions:

1. According to the speaker, what is the best way for one to learn about old people?
2. Why did the speaker feel that his experience with an old man of 80 was unusual and exciting?
3. Why can't the speaker meet people who are twice his age?
4. Where did the speaker's father go after he had a stroke?
5. What kind of relationship was there between the speaker's father and other people at the adult day center?
6. What is important to an person when he or she grows old according to the speaker?

Key

1. Meeting people who are already old.
2. Because the old man was the first one he spent time with outside his family.
3. Because the speaker himself has grown older.
4. He went to an adult day center.
5. People understood the speaker's father and accepted him as he was.
6. Having something new.

Notes

1. **the better part of a day**

   "The better part of something" means "more than half of something". In the talk, "the better part of a day" means "most of the time on that day".

2. **flea markets**

   A market, usually held outdoors, where used goods and antiques are sold. The term is a direct translation of the French marché aux *puces* [(法语)跳蚤], which probably came from the fact that some used clothes and furniture might have fleas in them.

3. Palm Springs

    Palm Springs is a resort city in southern California that is surrounded by desert and mountains. The city is named for the palm trees that line its streets and its natural hot springs.

4. Oldsmobile

    Olds, Ransom Eli（1864—1950）was an American pioneer automobile inventor and manufacturer. He introduced mass production to the automobile industry in 1901. Oldsmobile was a brand of automobile named for him.

5. This was liberating for him

    The word "liberating" is used as an adjective in this context. It means "making one feel free and able to behave as one likes".

Part D Dictation

Purpose

This part contains a short talk to be dictated to the students. This exercise trains the students' skills in writing down what they have heard.

Detailed Plan

1. Study the new words and expressions in *Word Bank*.
2. Listen to the short talk from the beginning to the end without any pause.
3. Write down the sentences during the pauses when the short talk is spoken again.
4. Read the listening script and correct whatever mistakes the students may have made.
5. Listen to the short talk again if necessary.

Listening Script

Directions：You will hear a short talk about global aging. The short talk will be spoken twice. After you listen to it at normal speed, the short talk will be spoken again with pauses. During the pauses, write down what you hear in the space provided below.

Population aging is a global phenomenon. By the year 2050, there will be 2 billion older persons in the world, compared to 600 million today. Every month, approximately 1 million persons reach 60 years of age.

Forecasts show that in 2050, the percentage of older persons will rise to 21 percent worldwide, up from 8 percent today, while the percentage of children will decline to 20 percent, from 33 percent today. The result is by the middle of this century, there will be more old people than children on Earth

大学英语自主听力指南4

for the first time in human history.

Part E   Fun Time

Listening Script

Directions: Listen twice to a humorous story about an elderly man who recovered his hearing. Retell the story to your classmates.

An elderly gentleman had serious hearing problems for a number of years.

He went to the doctor and the doctor was able to have him fitted for a set of hearing aids that allowed the gentleman to hear 100%.

The elderly gentleman went back in a month to the doctor and the doctor said, "Your hearing is perfect. Your family must be really pleased that you can hear again."

To which the gentleman said, "Oh, I haven't told my family yet. I just sit around and listen to the conversations. I've changed my will three times!"

Test Yourself (Units 1~8)

Section A

Listening Script and Key

Directions: In this section, you will hear 8 short conversations and 2 long conversations. At the end of each conversation, one or more questions will be asked about what was said. Both the conversation and the questions will be spoken only once. After each question there will be a pause. During the pause, you must read the four choices marked A, B, C and D, and decide which is the best answer.

1. Man: About 7,000 Americans study in Florence in some 40 study-abroad programs, and 80 percent of them are women.

   Woman: If I had such an opportunity, I would join them, too. When I was in France, I learned a lot about the French culture and almost became fluent in the language.

   Question: What does the woman want to do?

2. Woman: Why should people have an emergency fund?

   Man: Because when you don't have an emergency fund or an emergency savings account and something goes wrong, your only choice is to put it on a credit card. And then as we've seen with many people, it typically costs much more than the original emergency to pay it back.

   Question: According to the man, when something goes wrong, what does one have to do without an emergency fund?

3. Man: Thousands of people have lost their lives in the 911 terrorist attacks. How do you cope with losing a family member or somebody you love in such tragic and unexpected circumstances?

   Woman: Well, it's certainly one of those things that you cannot be prepared for in any way. You just have to rely on your friends and your family and your faith because that's when those things come to mean so much to you.

   Question: What does the woman think of the terrorist attacks?

4. Woman: Although music is usually a source of comfort in a time of crisis, I don't feel like listening to music these days.

   Man: Neither do I. The problem is that I'm not sure I want to be comforted. The day of the terrorist attack, I turned to poetry, not music.

   Question: Why don't the two speakers feel like listening to music these days?

5. Man: Well, as my mom used to say, there's no place like home. Could you tell us something about your hometown?

   Woman: Well, when people think of New York, they think Manhattan. But there are four other boroughs surrounding the city each with a unique style and flavor. My hometown is just north of Manhattan. Many have heard of it but few really know it.

   Question: What do you know about the woman's hometown?

6. Woman: Read enough of these, you start thinking history is filled with a lot of "what ifs" or "what might have beens." History is just random.

   Man: History is very random. And history, and especially military history, has to do with personal decisions time and again. And you have decisions of people in the field, and they have to make split-second decisions. And sometimes, those decisions which seem right then turn out not to be very good.

   Question: What does the man think of the decisions made by people in the field?

7. Man: Are you going to buy a car soon?

   Woman: Well, it won't be too much longer because my husband and I are both going to retire. When we retire we'll travel all over the country. We are going to buy us a new one and get rid of the two that we have right now.

   Question: What can we conclude from the conversation?

8. Woman: Today's public policy does not always reflect the proper concern for those who set the stage and paved the way for us.

   Man: You are absolutely right. I often wonder if we have forgotten that our elderly eat the same food, feel the same hurt, are subject to the same disease, healed by the same means and are warmed and cooled by the same weather.

   Question: What does the man think of today's public policy towards the aged?

Long Conversation 1

Woman: Do you ever tire of hearing people's problems?

Man: No ... never. I feel privileged to be in the position of possibly making a difference in the lives of so many people who are hurting, broken-hearted, laden with guilt or feeling helpless.

Woman: How do you remain so enthusiastic about your work and keep it fresh 365 days a year?

Man: I've never lost my enthusiasm because every day is different, and there are so many opportunities to help people of all ages ... from the high school sophomore who is downhearted to the adopted people wanting to find their "real" parents, to people who want me to support their decision to stop giving gifts to kids who don't send them a thank-you note.

Woman: What is the most difficult part about your job? The most rewarding?

Man: The most difficult part of my job is not having the time to carry on a correspondence with the thousands of people who write me. After I have solved one problem, they send me another. The most rewarding part is helping people see options they hadn't recognized, guiding readers to resources for help, or simply confirming that they have made the right decisions.

Woman: Is there any project you have been involved in of which you are particularly proud?

Man: "Operation Dear Abby," which created pen pals for men and women serving their country in foreign lands. Dear Abby readers of all ages — from teenagers to men and women in nursing homes — correspond as a result of that program.

Questions 9 to 11 are based on the conversation you have just heard.

9. Who is the man in the conversation?

10. What is the most difficult part of the man's job?

11. Why is the man proud of his "Operation Dear Abby" project?

Long Conversation 2

Man: Alice, you've had such an amazing influence on food in America for so many years. Did you know from an early age that you wanted to be a chef?

Woman: No, not at all. When I was 19, I was a student living in France. My home was on the other side of a farmer's market and I walked through that market every day on my way to school. When I came back to California, I wanted those same foodstuffs here. Unfortunately, it took a long time to develop a local farming system to produce and support fresh, local ingredients.

Man: What sort of ingredients were missing? It seems we have an abundance of produce in Northern California.

Woman: Unusual ingredients. I started shopping at Chinese markets in Berkeley and also soliciting produce from nearby gardens.

Man: I remember reading that President Clinton had dinner at one of your restaurants called Chez Panisse years ago. That must have been a nerve-wracking experience.

Woman: Yes, it certainly was but I've cooked for him outside of the restaurant as well. You know, I also wrote President Clinton several letters stressing the need for a sustainable agriculture as the backbone to a strong community. We need more families sitting down and eating dinner together.

Man: For those who aren't familiar with your food, how would you describe your style?

Woman: Well, it's definitely Mediterranean-inspired. Simple, straight-forward food incorporating olive oil, vegetables, and grains. We pair it with French and sometimes Spanish or Italian wine.

Questions 12 to 15 are based on the conversation you have just heard.

12. What influenced Alice in her decision of becoming a chef in America?

13. How did the woman feel when Clinton had dinner at one of her restaurants?

14. According to the woman, what is an effective way to strengthen the community in the US?

15. What is the style of the Alice's cooking?

Key

1. D 2. A 3. A 4. D 5. D 6. C 7. C 8. B 9. C 10. D 11. A 12. C 13. B 14. D 15. A

Section B

Directions: In this section, you will hear 3 short passages. At the end of each passage, you will hear some questions. Both the passage and the questions will be spoken only once. After you hear a question, you must choose the best answer from the four choices marked A, B, C and D.

Passage One

I just bought a second-hand car for my oldest daughter, a red Honda Civic. My ex-husband, Dwayne, helped out physically and financially.

In Southern California. Cars figure in nearly every memory of our lives together. For the most part, my ex-husband doesn't even remember names, but connects friends and acquaintances with their vehicles. He'll say to me, I saw your old friend today, the one that used to drive the Duster. Ah, I'll reply, Julie. She drove a Duster in 1978.

When we began dating, he was just 16 and I was 15. The first time Dwayne drove up to my house, I saw a 1960 Cadillac. I noticed a dark stain inside the driver's door. It was cold, and I asked him to close his window, but he couldn't. He didn't want me to see the spider web cracks around the bullet hole in the glass.

We never had much money growing up, but Dwayne and I tell our girls some good stories, and they all involve cars. We tell them about how we drove with eight bodies packed into our friend Penguin's Dodge Dart. At our wedding we had no limo. So Dwayne's cousin drove us around the local lake in his Cadillac, which had a broken horn. The best man shouted out the open windows to waving onlookers. Honk, honk, dang it, these people just got married.

Well, now we're not married. And when we drove home from the yard where we had partied years ago and where we bought the Honda, I realized how our stories still matched up. Our daughters had seen us disagree over plenty of things, but not our past.

Questions 16 to 18 are based on the passage you have just heard.

16. While the speaker's ex-husband Dwayne cannot remember the names, how is he able to tell the speaker who he has met?
17. Why didn't Dwayne close the car window when the speaker asked him to do it?
18. What car did the speaker and Dwayne take on their wedding day?

Passage Two

George and Matilda had their youngest child Sally in 1930. Sally remembers the huge dinners they'd had in the dining room and the large living room there was closed most of the time. She lived there in the heart of Detroit until she married in 1951. By then, many of the family she had grown up with had begun moving to the suburbs. Her parents held onto their home. But when George died, Matilda finally agreed to sell the house in 1970.

In 1988, two African-American lawyers, Ed and Florice Ewell, found themselves planning their wedding and looking for a house at the same time. They bought the house for $250,000 and settled in to raise their children in what had become one of the city's many purposely integrated neighborhoods. Florice had no idea why the house had been built or who had lived there before, but she always felt there was a spirit of love and family that filled the rooms. When asked whether the house had ghosts, Florice once said, "No. It's full of angels."

Last year Florice put her house on a neighborhood home tour. She discovered that a member of the family who built the house was still alive. Sally hadn't been in her childhood home for 30 years, so

Florice extended an invitation.

Sally arrived on an unseasonably warm winter day, barely able to contain her wonder. "I broke my front tooth on these steps," Sally said. Once inside she grew teary. "I used to get stuck in this bathroom," she said. "The door was so heavy I couldn't push it open."

"That happens to my daughter, too," Florice said with a laugh.

As Sally and Florice settled on the sofa to swap photos and memories of the great house, they could have been relatives, not perfect strangers. "It's so different," Sally said of the house she knew so well, "but it's still home."

Questions 19 to 21 are based on the passage you have just heard.
19. How long did Sally live in the big house?
20. How did the Ewells feel while living in the house?
21. Why did Sally get stuck in the bathroom when she was young?

Passage Three

Ringling brothers were five brothers who founded the most famous circus in American entertainment history. The brothers were Albert, Otto, Alfred, Charles, and John. Their dedication and organizational skills helped build a small group of performers into one of the greatest circuses in the world.

The Ringlings were the sons of a harness maker from Germany. Albert was born in Chicago, Otto in Baraboo, Wis., and Alfred, Charles, and John in McGregor, Iowa. In 1884, the brothers started a traveling circus. At the time, there were a number of circuses touring the United States, including the huge Barnum show that traveled on 60 railroad cars. The Ringlings had little money for equipment or performers, so they did most of the work themselves. They held their first performance on May 19, 1884, in Baraboo. The brothers and 17 other employees sewed and pitched the tent, sold tickets, played in the band, and performed the acts.

Two other brothers, Henry and August, joined the Ringling circus later in the 1880's. Each of the seven brothers was responsible for one aspect of the circus management. The brothers invested almost all the profits back into the circus, which grew rapidly. At first, they took their show from town to town in wagons pulled by horses. By 1890, the circus traveled by railroad. The Ringlings soon became strong competitors of the Barnum & Bailey circus, the largest circus of the time. In 1907, the Ringlings purchased the Barnum & Bailey circus, but the two shows toured separately until 1919. That year, they merged to form the Ringling Brothers and Barnum & Bailey Circus. The Ringling family sold the circus in 1967, but the new owners kept the name.

Questions 22 to 25 are based on the passage you have just heard.
22. Where did the Ringlings' father come from?
23. How many people were there in the Ringlings' circus at first?
24. What did the Ringlings do with their money that they earned from their performances in the 1880's?
25. What is the passage mainly about?

Key

16. A 17. C 18. D 19. A 20. B 21. B 22. B 23. C 24. C 25. D

Section C

Directions: In this section, you will hear a passage three times. When the passage is read for the first time, you should listen carefully for its general idea. When the passage is read for the second time, you are required to fill in the blanks numbered from 26 to 33 with the exact words you have just heard. For blanks numbered from 34 to 36 you are required to fill in the missing information. For these blanks, you can either use the exact words you have just heard or write down the main points in your own words. Finally, when the passage is read for the third time, you should check what you have written.

Cable television delivers signals to home TV sets through cables. It has two important <u>advantages</u> over commercial and public television. First, it <u>offers</u> improved reception of network and local station programs. Second, it provides a greater <u>variety</u> of programming.

Cable television was first used in the late 1940's. Its <u>original</u> purpose was to bring network and local programs to places that cannot receive TV signals through the air. Such places include <u>isolated</u> communities, mountain valleys, extremely <u>hilly</u> regions, and areas with many tall buildings.

Improved reception of <u>regular</u> television programs still ranks as an important purpose of cable television. But since the <u>1960's</u>, people have begun to use it for other purposes. Some cable systems carry more than 100 channels — <u>far more than can be broadcast over the airwaves</u> even in the largest urban areas. This increase in the number of channels available has made narrowcasting possible. Unlike broadcasting, <u>which tries to appeal to the largest possible audience</u>, narrowcasting offers programs that appeal to a particular age, ethnic, or interest group. For example, cable channels may specialize in movies, news, sports, music, comedy, health, religion, weather, or Spanish-language programs. <u>Such channels focus on attracting viewers with particular interests</u>. Thus, cable television offers a wide variety of programming to its viewers.

Key

26. advantages   27. offers   28. variety   29. original   30. isolated   31. hilly   32. regular
33. 1960's
34. far more than can be broadcast over the airwaves
35. which tries to appeal to the largest possible audience
36. Such channels focus on attracting viewers with particular interests

Unit 9

Growing Pains

Preview

This unit integrates various useful expressions and authentic talks about growing pains.

Objectives

After studying this unit, the students are expected to:
1. know the basic words and expressions about growing pains;
2. understand conversations and short talks about different ways to express growing pains;
3. be able to make brief comments on growing pains.

Part A Language Focus

Note

adolescents & adolescence

An adolescent is a young person, usually between the ages of 12 and 18, who is developing into an adult.

The adolescent grows up to become the adult. The words "adolescent" and "adult" come from forms of the same Latin word, adolēscere, meaning "to grow up." The present participle of adolēscere, adolēscēns, from which adolescent derives, means "growing up," while the past participle adultus, the source of adult, means "grown up."

Adolescence is the time in a young person's life between childhood and adulthood. It starts when a person is about 12 years old and ends at about the age of 19.

Adolescence is a time of great change. Changes in adolescents' bodies are quite visible as boys begin to grow facial hair and their voices deepen while girls grow breasts and wider hips. They also experience changes in their emotions, or feelings, as well as their thoughts and beliefs. They often see the world differently, and they act differently than they did when they were children.

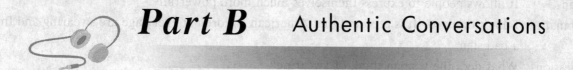

Part B Authentic Conversations

Purpose

This part aims to familiarize the students with authentic conversations that can be heard in our daily life about growing pains.

Detailed Plan

1. Study the new words and expressions in *Word Bank*.
2. Do the required exercises.
3. Check the answers.
4. Listen to the conversations again. Pay special attention to the parts you didn't understand or misunderstood. You may refer to the script if necessary.

Short Conversations

Listening Script

Directions: You will hear 6 conversations between two speakers. Listen to them and answer the following questions by choosing the right options.

1. Man: Tell me what are some of the things that you did with your children when they were growing up.

    Woman: Oh, well, uh, when they were little we did lots of reading, playing, and going to parks, and things of that sort.

    Question: Which of the following is not true?

2. Woman: I have three boys. They are swimmers and so, as they were growing up, much of our normal life revolved around their swimming.

Man: Oh, well, that's good. Mine were not terribly sporting. Uh, they did both T-ball and soccer in junior high schools. But neither one of them carried on the sports after that.

Question: Which sport did the woman's children do?

3. Man: Many kids said swearing was useful.

Woman: Why is it useful?

Man: It allows people to express themselves much more powerfully.

Woman: I don't think so. It is reported that American children at every age are swearing and that's a bad sign.

Question: What does the woman think of swearing?

4. Woman: Where do you eat lunch and dinner?

Man: I usually don't eat lunch or dinner.

Woman: You don't? Why are you on the streets?

Man: Because my mother kicked me out when I was 9 years old and I went to live with one of my friends out in Colorado for four years, and then I moved back home for about two months and then my mom kicked me out again.

Question: Why is the man on the streets?

5. Man: Are teenagers' eating habits much worse today than they were, say, 10, or 20 years ago?

Woman: The evidence is that we're eating more. We're eating more sugar, starch, and fat. We're not exercising enough, all of the things that we know contribute to obesity. I think the answer is yes.

Man: I guess parents should set a good example as well.

Woman: There's no question that if you are a good role model, it'll help your teenager to do better.

Question: According to the woman, which of the following is true about teenagers today?

6. Man: It comes as no surprise that teenagers are risky drivers, but what specific risks did you find that the teenagers are taking?

Woman: We were particularly interested to find that not only teenagers who had been involved in serious crashes, but also those who had never been involved in a crash were reporting to us that they engaged in behaviors such as passing two or three cars at a time on a two-lane road or driving more than 20 miles an hour over the speed limit.

Question: What are the speakers talking about?

Key

1. D 2. B 3. C 4. A 5. B 6. C

Notes

> **1. Colorado**
> Colorado is a state in the western United States. It is located in the Rocky Mountain region.

2. teen obesity

Teen obesity has grown to epidemic proportions in the United States. According to statistics, 14% of adolescents in the United States are overweight. This figure has nearly tripled in the last 20 years.

3. teen driving

In general the driving age in North America is 16, but it can be as low as 14 (in rural areas, and usually for farm equipment only) or as old as 19. Most states and provinces require parental consent in order for teens to get a driver's license before 18.

Longer Conversations

Conversation One

Listening Script

Directions: You will hear a conversation between two speakers. Listen to the conversation twice and answer the questions by choosing the right options.

Man: It may be surprising, but 64 percent of college students have a credit card. You can help your kids learn to use it wisely by doing something as simple as going over your monthly statement the year before they leave home.

Woman: Money problems are severe, and left unchecked, they become adult money problems. And they just keep growing and growing. Deal with it when they're younger, when you can still help them.

Man: Well, that's a great idea, to have your parents — have the parents flak to the kids. But you know, sometimes the kids don't want to listen. The good news for parents is that schools are now getting involved a little bit, with bankruptcies up 300 percent since 1980, more schools across the country have begun to require courses on money management. And in the 26 states where such courses are mandatory, the average young person saves 5 percent more than in states that don't have the programs. So the good news is, money management can be taught if kids learn to listen.

Woman: Just got to get their attention.

Man: Exactly.

Questions:

1. In the man's opinion, what can parents do to help young people to use their credit cards wisely?
2. What does the woman think of money problems among college students?
3. What have schools done in order to help young people deal with money problems?
4. According to the woman, what is the use of the courses on money management?

Key

1. C 2. A 3. C 4. D

Notes

1. monthly statement

This is an account statement mailed or sent by electronic mail to a customer that lists debits, credits, service charges, and account adjustments during the prior month.

2. money management

The process of budgeting, saving, investing, spending or otherwise in overseeing the cash usage of an individual or group.

In today's money-driven society, teens are constantly bombarded by magazines, television ads, and peer pressure which make them feel less than ideal if they do not wear the latest clothing style and drive a "cool" car. However, with parents and schools' help, it is possible to raise teens with money sense and save them from making serious financial mistakes.

Conversation Two

Listening Script

Directions: You will hear a conversation between two speakers. Listen to the conversation twice and write your answers to the questions in the space provided below.

Man: Good morning, Sabrina.

Woman: Good morning.

Man: You talked to thousands and thousands of teenagers. And in your recent book about teens you make a great comparison between the parents getting them ready for driving and sex.

Woman: Yes, that's right. Driving is a very dangerous activity that we know most teens are going to do, but parents give teens so much preparation for driving — they practice, they talk about it — whereas with sex, it's equally dangerous, if not even more so. And the conversation is just not keeping up with teenagers' reality.

Man: In fact talking about the birds and the bees can be a very tough conversation.

Woman: But it is so important to get the subject out in the open. Parents are actually the most influential factors in teens' decisions about sex. Teens want to hear from their parents about sex and what they need to do.

Questions:

1. What did the woman frequently do in the past?
2. According to the woman, what are the two very dangerous activities for teenagers?
3. For what do parents give teens much preparation?
4. What does "talking about the birds and the bees" mean in the conversation?
5. Why don't parents talk about sex to teenagers as much as they should?
6. What do teens want to hear from their parents?

Key

1. She talked to thousands and thousands of teenagers.
2. Driving and sex.
3. They give teens much preparation for driving.
4. It means "talking about sex."
5. Because it is a tough topic.
6. They want to hear from their parents about sex and what they need to do.

Note

> **the birds and the bees**
>
> "The birds and the bees" (sometimes expanded to "the birds, the bees and the butterflies" or "the birds, the bees, the flowers, and the trees") is an idiomatic expression which refers to courtship and sex, and is usually used in reference to teaching a young child about sex and pregnancy. The phrase is a *euphemism* (委婉语) often used to avoid speaking openly and technically about the subject.

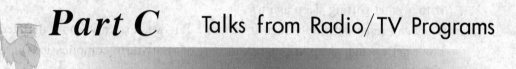

Part C Talks from Radio/TV Programs

Purpose

This part consists of exercises based on talks excerpted from radio/TV programs. The students are expected to understand such talks and get the necessary information from them.

Detailed Plan

1. Study the new words and expressions in *Word Bank*.
2. Do the exercises based on *Excerpt One* and *Excerpt Two*.
3. Check the answers.
4. Listen to the short talks again. Pay special attention to the parts you didn't understand or misunderstood. You may refer to the script if necessary.

Excerpt One

Listening Script

Directions: You will hear a short talk from a TV program. Listen to it twice and decide whether the following statements are true (T) or false (F) according to the short talk.

Thomson (Host): Good morning, Doctor.

Findlay (Doctor): Good morning.

Thomson: Teens stay up late. And they do all kinds of — there's a range of different things that they would have been going on in the day as to why they may not get as much sleep as they need. But how do you tell if it's just an average day and maybe they need a little bit more sleep, or it's actually a chronic problem?

Findlay: Well, I think for some teenagers it's something that just occurs now and again. And they fix it pretty quickly. But for other teenagers it does become sort of a chronic problem where they become sleep-deprived over the course of weeks and months. And it really does affect their functioning in many ways.

Thomson: Is there a benchmark as to how many hours — like, just in general — that a teenager should get?

Findlay: The recommendation is at least eight, and for some teenagers really nine or ten hours is what's needed for them to be functioning at their best.

Thomson: For the teenagers who were sleep-deprived, is it something that they can turn around if they start getting sleep again?

Findlay: They can most definitely turn it around. But we certainly know that teenagers who don't get enough sleep are at risk of sort of short-term complications in terms of not doing as well in school as they can. They're more likely to develop mental-health problems, particularly depression as well.

Thomson: Thank you very much for joining us, doctor.

Findlay: Thank you.

Key

1. T   2. F   3. T   4. F   5. T   6. T

Note

teens' sleep problem

Teens can have sleep problems just like adults. Often the biggest problem facing a teenager is not getting enough sleep. It is now well-known that being sleep-deprived can lead to behavioral problems in school, so it is important that teens get enough sleep.

Excerpt Two

Listening Script

Directions: You will hear a short talk from a radio program. Listen to it twice and write your answers to the questions in the space provided below.

Alphonso Van Marsh: Snack time at Connor McCreedy's house. And weighing in at around 200 pounds, Connor is relishing every bite. A chicken drumstick may seem typical for a young kid. But Connor is just eight years old. Almost four times the average weight for a kid his age. Connor's mother says she's obliged to answer her son's constant demands for more food, but British authorities say they're very concerned that the diet he's being fed can seriously damage his health.

Nicola McKeown, Mother: If I'd neglected Connor, he would be a skinny kid, a skinny little runt.

Van Marsh: On a typical day, Connor starts with a bowl of chocolate cereal, followed by some toast, with processed meat. Lunchtime means a burger and fries and sausages or a pizza, a whole pizza. It's fast food takeaway for dinner. And toss in four bags of potato chips. And Connor's family admits that in addition to all of that, he scarves down cookies and other snacks about every 20 minutes.

British social services had a hearing with Connor's mother and grandmother Tuesday and decided the child can stay at home for now. In a statement, social services says it's made a formal agreement with the family to, quote, "safeguard and promote the child's welfare."

Questions:

1. How much does the fat boy weigh?
2. How old is the fat boy?
3. What do British authorities think of the boy's diet?
4. What does the boy's mother think of the way the boy is raised at home?
5. What does the boy typically eat at lunch?
6. What does the boy eat every 20 minutes during the day?
7. What does British Social Services want the boy's family to do?

Key

1. 200 pounds.
2. 8.
3. It could seriously damage his health.
4. She believes that she is taking good care of the boy.
5. He eats a burger, fries, sausages or a whole pizza.
6. Cookies and snacks.
7. To safeguard and promote the child's welfare.

Notes

1. **burger**

   A burger can mean a hamburger or other finely chopped fish, vegetables, nuts, etc. made into flat round shapes like hamburgers.

2. **fries**

   Also called French fries, fries are thin strips of potato fried in deep fat.

3. social services

Social services refers to the parts of social security requiring individual contact rather than cash payments. People's minimum consumption needs can be met by cash payments to those without sufficient incomes, through pensions and other benefits. Some citizens, however, need personal assistance with managing their lives as well as cash handouts. Personal social services cover matters such as home help for the disabled, advice and supervision for those on probation, advice and assistance in dealing with children and adults with behavioral problems, and supervision of parents thought to be in danger of harming their children.

Part D Dictation

Purpose

This part contains a short talk to be dictated to the students. This exercise trains the students' skills in writing down what they have heard.

Detailed Plan

1. Study the new words and expressions in *Word Bank*.
2. Listen to the short talk from the beginning to the end without any pause.
3. Write down the sentences during the pauses when the short talk is spoken again.
4. Read the listening script and correct whatever mistakes the learners may have made.
5. Listen to the short talk again if necessary.

Listening Script

Directions: You will hear a short talk about a boy called Espen. The short talk will be spoken twice. After you listen to it at normal speed, the short talk will be spoken again with pauses. During the pauses, write down what you hear in the space provided below.

My son Espen turns 13 next week. He seemed to be a sensitive soul with a good heart. That was when he was in the first grade, and my opinion has not changed.

In every other way, though, he has changed.

I appear to be shrinking and he appears to be growing. He can wear my ski boots and socks. He can ski faster than I. He can reach shelves. He has responsibilities.

But I don't know exactly what my son is thinking, ever.

Part E   Fun Time

Listening Script

Directions: Listen twice to a dialogue between a girl and a boy. Tell why the boy's mother would give
him extra pocket money every week.

Girl: What did you get for Christmas?

Boy: A mouth organ. It's the best present I've ever had.

Girl: Why?

Boy: My mum gives me extra pocket money every week not to play it!

Note

My mum gives me extra pocket money every week not to play it!
Apparently the boy's mother does not like to hear the noise the boy makes at home.

Technology

Preview

This unit integrates various useful expressions and authentic talks about technology.

Objectives

After studying this unit, the students are expected to:
1. know the basic words and expressions about science and technology;
2. understand conversations and short talks about science and technology;
3. be able to make brief comments on various aspects of technology.

Part A   Language Focus

Note

science, technique, technology

Science is the study of phenomena, aimed at discovering enduring principles of the world by employing formal techniques such as the scientific method. A technique is a procedure used to accomplish a specific activity or task. Technology is a broad concept dealing with the use of materials, tools, techniques, and sources of power to make life easier or more pleasant and work more productive.

e.g. There are various techniques for dealing with industrial pollution.
The scientists call the age we live in the age of technology.

Part B   Authentic Conversations

Purpose

This part aims to familiarize the students with authentic conversations that can be heard in our daily life about technology.

Detailed Plan

1. Study the new words and expressions in *Word Bank*.
2. Do the required exercises.
3. Check the answers.
4. Listen to the conversations again. Pay special attention to the parts you didn't understand or misunderstood. You may refer to the script if necessary.

Short Conversations

Listening Script

Directions: You will hear 6 conversations between two speakers. Listen to them and answer the following questions by choosing the right options.

1. Woman: How do you program a robot to recognize a face?

   Man: Being able to recognize the difference between a dog and a cat reliably, every 2-year-old kid can do it. No machine can do it.

   Question: What does the man mean?

2. Man: Education has always been a big focus for you. So, is there better learning through technology?

   Woman: Learning is mostly about motivating the learners in a learning environment. Technology plays a role, but it's not a panacea.

   Question: What is the woman's opinion of the role of technology in education?

3. Man: My computer is constantly interrupting me with reminders to update programs that I don't even use. Is there an easy way to shut it down?

   Woman: It depends on the program. Actually you don't have to find the setting to turn off the update warnings. I would advise leaving the update warnings on, but perhaps set them to appear less frequently.

Question: What does the woman advise?

4. Man: I think that the idea that everything that's done in a scientific laboratory needs to have some kind of direct application to social needs is an extremely dangerous position for our society to take.

Woman: Yes, if we invest solely in those aspects of our science that have immediate applications, it won't be very long before we have very little new knowledge to apply.

Question: Which of the following statements would the speakers most probably agree with?

5. Woman: I think it probably would be more prudent for me to drive my car on a trip rather than fly.

Man: If you really have an understanding of technology, you have a much greater chance of being in an accident and being injured if you're in a car than you are if you're on an airplane.

Question: What does the man imply?

6. Woman: A lot of scientists are worried that robots could get too refined and too intelligent. But why are they still working so hard on developing great robots?

Man: The experts say that you got to treat robot technology sort of like children. It's true that some might grow up to be criminals, but that doesn't mean we stop having them. So, the idea here is to develop the technology in a way that it's intelligent and safe.

Question: In what way is a robot similar to a child according to the man?

Key

1. B　2. D　3. D　4. C　5. A　6. A

Note

robot

A robot is a mechanical device that operates automatically. Robots can perform a wide variety of tasks. They are especially suitable for doing jobs too boring, difficult, or dangerous for people. A typical robot performs a task by following a set of instructions that specifies exactly what must be done to complete the job. These instructions are entered and stored in the robot's control center, which consists of a computer or part of a computer.

Longer Conversations

Conversation One

Listening Script

Directions: You will hear a conversation between two speakers. Listen to the conversation twice and answer the questions by choosing the right options.

Corley: Imagine trying to function without your cell phone or MP3 player. Could you do it? Well, journalism professor Danna Walker assigned a 24-hour electronic media fast, which meant her students couldn't consume anything electronic. Professor Walker joins us in the studio today to tell us how it went. Welcome.

Walker: Thank you.

Corley: All right. Well, Dr. Walker, tell us first how you got this idea.

Walker: I'd like to say that it hit me like a bolt of lightning, but I had actually read about it in a book which mentioned that there was another professor in the country who had done this.

Corley: Do you know which device was the hardest for the students to give up?

Walker: I thought that it would be the cell phone. But I was surprised. Many students are totally tied to their computers. Others almost couldn't function without their cell phones. And others really missed just watching TV.

Corley: What did the students tell you they ended up doing during those 24 hours?

Walker: Some went out to eat a lot, and played board games with their families. Some worked in the yard. I had one student who actually bought a newspaper. Most of them tried to sleep as much as they could.

Corley: What do you think this experiment says about our society?

Walker: It told me that we're all really hooked in to electronic media. What got me thinking about it a lot was that when I was teaching and talking about different types of media, I realized that my students didn't think of it that way. It's all one big media world. And so I think by doing the e-media fast, they were able to differentiate more between media.

Questions:

1. Where did Prof. Walker get the idea of a 24-hour electronic media fast?
2. What did Prof. Walker think was the hardest for the students to give up before the experiment?
3. What did the students do most during the 24 hours?
4. What did Prof. Walker think the students were able to do after the electronic media fast?

Key

1. B   2. C   3. A   4. C

Note

MP3 player

    MP3 player is a digital music player that supports the MP3 format, a computer file standard for downloading compressed music from the Internet, playable on a multimedia computer with appropriate software.

Conversation Two

Listening Script

Directions: You will hear a conversation between two speakers. Listen to the conversation twice and write your answers to the questions in the space provided below.

Flatow: How would you define what technology is, Dr. Wulf?

Dr. Wulf: OK. You know, we use the word "science" in two different ways. We use it to describe the body of facts that we know about nature. We also use it to describe the process by which we discover those facts. In the case of engineering and technology, we use two different words. Technology is the body of knowledge about physically constructed and human-constructed objects. And engineering is the word we use to describe the process.

Flatow: Is that how most people define technology? Didn't you ask people in your poll to define technology?

Dr. Wulf: Yes. But most of the people that we asked, two-thirds of them, said that technology was primarily computers and the Internet. So that was kind of an alarming finding for us.

Flatow: Can you give us some highlights of the poll? What did you find out about what Americans think technology is?

Dr. Wulf: Well, the primary purpose of the poll was to provide information on how Americans felt about technology and education. There were two major findings. We've already talked about one, which is the public's definition of technology as a narrow one, encompassing mostly computers and the Internet. But the other one was very positive. There's an overwhelming agreement — 97 percent — by the public that schools should include the study of technology in the curriculum.

Questions:

1. What does the word "science" refer to?
2. How does Dr. Wulf define technology?
3. What was the public's definition of technology according to Dr. Wulf's poll?
4. What is the primary purpose of the poll?
5. What does the public agree on?

Key

1. It refers to the body of facts about nature and the process of discovering those facts.
2. It is the body of knowledge about physically constructed and human-constructed objects.
3. It was primarily computers and the Internet.
4. To provide information on how Americans felt about technology and education.
5. Schools should include the study of technology in the curriculum.

Part C   Talks from Radio/TV Programs

Purpose

This part consists of exercises based on talks excerpted from radio/TV programs. The students are expected to understand such talks and get the necessary information from them.

Detailed Plan

1. Study the new words and expressions in *Word Bank*.
2. Do the exercises based on *Excerpt One* and *Excerpt Two*.
3. Check the answers.
4. Listen to the short talks again. Pay special attention to the parts you didn't understand or misunderstood. You may refer to the script if necessary.

Excerpt One

Listening Script

Directions: You will hear a short talk from a radio program. Listen to it twice and decide whether the following statements are true (T) or false (F) according to the short talk.

    Looking at the world around us today with space exploration, medicines and electronic gadgets of all kinds, it would be easy to assume that humans have innovated and improved things constantly throughout history pushed by some innate drive, but that hasn't been the case. For the vast majority of human history, important technological innovations were actually quite uncommon. The earliest human tools seem to have satisfied people for almost a million years, and then there was the next great leap to something called a hand ax, which in turn remained unchanged for 700,000 years. It is not that humans aren't naturally innovative. Just look at the development of language. And for thousands of years, people have expressed creativity through music, culture and storytelling, but there wasn't the constant pursuit of technological innovation that we see today. In part, that's because as the pace of innovation picked up, it often met resistance. Also scientific pursuits were removed from common people. Even just a few hundred years ago most people saw no technological progress during their entire lives and kept farming or making pottery the same way their parents did.

Key

1. F 2. T 3. F 4. T 5. T 6. F

Excerpt Two

Listening Script

Directions: You will hear a short talk from a TV program. Listen to it twice and answer the questions by choosing the right options.

M. O'Brien: The hardest thing about making an atomic bomb isn't building the bomb itself; it's producing the nuclear fuel.

David Albright: The tall pole in the tent is certainly getting the capability to make the highly enriched uranium. It's not simple to make nuclear weapons; it's simpler than learning to build and operate gas centrifuges.

M. O'Brien: Uranium is like crude oil; it must first be refined before it becomes fuel. And the refinery is called a centrifuge.

Imagine, for a moment, this bag of M & M's is a package of uranium. Now, they're all M & M's, or all uranium atoms in this case, but there are different kinds. As a matter of fact, there are three different kinds of uranium, but only one. In this case, for our example, let's call them the blue M & M's. Only one is useful if you're trying to generate electricity or make a nuclear bomb. So the real question is, how do you separate the blue M & M's from all of the others? It's possible when you consider this one key point. Uranium 235, blue M & M's in this case, are ever so slightly lighter than the rest. So if it's possible to spin the tray, the heavier items move to the outside, the lighter stuff, the stuff you want, can stay in the middle

This is, in essence, what happens inside a centrifuge. Now imagine what happens when this is repeated over and over again.

That is what happened when a series of centrifuges is linked together. They call it a cascade. The uranium in gaseous form is piped from centrifuge to centrifuge, gets spun, and then respun again and again and again. Each time the uranium 235 content goes up, at 20 percent, it's good enough to run a nuclear power plant. Eighty percent uranium 235 is the high-test, the weapon's grade fuel.

Questions:

1. What is the hardest thing about making an atomic bomb?
2. In what way is uranium like crude oil?
3. Why does the speaker talk about M & M's?
4. How many kinds of uranium are there that can be used to make nuclear bombs?
5. What is the main function of a centrifuge?
6. At what percentage is uranium 235 good enough to run a nuclear power plant?

Key

1. C 2. A 3. C 4. A 5. D 6. B

Notes

> **1. The tall pole in the tent . . .**
>
> This expression is typically used to describe the lengthiest or most critical task in a project.
>
> *e.g. Getting funding is the tall pole in the tent for our launch.*
>
> **2. It's not simple to make nuclear weapons; it's simpler than learning to build and operate gas centrifuges.**
>
> The speaker means that making nuclear weapons is not easy, but it is comparatively easier or simpler than learning to build and operate gas centrifuges. In other words, building and operating gas centrifuges is more difficult than making nuclear weapons itself.
>
> **3. M&M's**
>
> M&M's chocolate candies are candy-coated pieces of chocolate with the letter "m" inscribed on them, produced by Mars, Incorporated.

Part D Dictation

Purpose

This part contains a short talk to be dictated to the students. This exercise trains the students' skills in writing down what they have heard.

Detailed Plan

1. Study the new words and expressions in *Word Bank*.
2. Listen to the short talk from the beginning to the end without any pause.
3. Write down the sentences during the pauses when the short talk is spoken again.
4. Read the listening script and correct whatever mistakes the students may have made.
5. Listen to the short talk again if necessary.

Listening Script

Directions: You will hear a short talk about industrial technology. The short talk will be spoken twice. After you listen to it at normal speed, the short talk will be spoken again with pauses. During the pauses, write down what you hear in the space provided below.

Industrial technology began about 200 years ago with the mass production of goods. As industrial technology advanced, it affected more and more aspects of people's lives. For example, the development of the automobile influenced where people lived and worked and how they spent their leisure time. Radio and television changed entertainment habits, and the telephone revolutionized communication. Today, industrial technology helps people achieve goals that few thought possible a hundred years ago.

Part E Fun Time

Listening Script

Directions: Listen twice to a humorous story about a computer technician and a user. Retell the story to your classmates and work out the misunderstanding.

One day an IBM office technician got a call from a user. The user cried for help as her new desktop computer was doing nothing.

"No problem," the IBM technician said. He told her to first open a "window" to launch a specific program.

The conversation continued, and the caller asked a few moments later if it might be all right for her to close the window.

"Why?" the IBM technician asked. Because, the caller responded, "it was getting very cold."

Note

IBM

IBM stands for International Business Machines Corporation, which is the world's largest manufacturer of information systems and equipment headquartered in New York, US. IBM produces mainframe computers, computer storage systems, and devices that connect to computers. The company also offers computer services that help customers develop and operate information systems. In addition, IBM develops software products for business applications.

Newspapers

Preview

This unit integrates various useful expressions and authentic talks about newspapers.

Objectives

After studying this unit, the students are expected to:
1. know the basic words and expressions about newspapers;
2. understand conversations and short talks about different ways to talk about newspapers;
3. be able to make brief comments on newspapers.

Part A   Language Focus

Notes

1. **tabloid**
    A tabloid is a small-format popular newspaper with a simple style, many photographs, and sometimes an emphasis on sensational stories.
2. *The Sun*
    The Sun is a tabloid daily newspaper published in the United Kingdom and the Republic of Ireland with the highest circulation of any daily English-language newspaper in the world.
3. *Daily Mail*
    The *Daily Mail* is a British newspaper, a tabloid, first published in 1896. It is Britain's

second biggest-selling daily newspaper after *The Sun*.

4. **Daily Express**

The *Daily Express* is a conservative, middle-market British tabloid newspaper. It is currently owned by Richard Desmond.

5. **The Times**

The Times is a daily national newspaper published in the United Kingdom since 1785. *The Times* is published by Times Newspapers Limited.

6. **The Guardian**

The Guardian (until 1959, The Manchester Guardian) is a British newspaper owned by the Guardian Media Group.

7. **USA Today**

USA Today is the No. 1 daily newspaper in the US, with a circulation of 2.3 million. The paper, first published in 1982, is available throughout the country and through international editions; it also publishes news on its popular website.

8. **The Wall Street Journal**

The Wall Street Journal is an international daily newspaper published in New York City with Asian and European editions. It has a worldwide daily circulation of more than 2 million.

9. **The New York Times**

The New York Times is one of the world's best-known newspapers. It is published daily in New York City and is distributed throughout the United States. The paper provides broad coverage of national and international news. *The Times* is also the nation's leading reference newspaper.

10. **Los Angeles Times**

The *Los Angeles Times* is a daily newspaper published in Los Angeles, California and distributed throughout the Western United States. It is the second-largest metropolitan newspaper in the United States. It has won 37 Pulitzer Prizes through 2004.

11. **The Washington Post**

The Washington Post is the largest and most circulated newspaper in Washington, D.C. It is widely considered to be one of the most important newspapers in the United States.

Part B Authentic Conversations

Purpose

This part aims to familiarize the students with authentic conversations that can be heard in our daily life about newspapers.

Detailed Plan

1. Study the new words and expressions in *Word Bank*.
2. Do the required exercises.
3. Check the answers.
4. Listen to the conversations again. Pay special attention to the parts you didn't understand or misunderstood. You may refer to the script if necessary.

Short Conversations

Listening Script

Directions: You will hear 6 conversations between two speakers. Listen to them and answer the following questions by choosing the right options.

1. Man: What papers do you subscribe to?

   Woman: In addition to *Newsday*, *The New York Times*, *The Wall Street Journal*, *The New York Post*, *the New York Daily News* and *USA Today*.

   Question: How many newspapers does the woman subscribe to?

2. Woman: I've never seen my 14-year-old stepdaughter read a newspaper. What can the industry do to change that?

   Man: I think the industry can make sure that good parents like you help their children read it every day.

   Question: What does the man mean?

3. Man: What newspaper do you read in Dallas?

   Woman: Uh, we have the *Dallas Times Herald* and the *Dallas Morning News*, but I don't read newspapers.

   Man: Don't you? How come?

   Woman: Huh, I have found it hard to follow from one page to another. It's just something I have never developed an interest in.

   Question: Which of the following is true about the woman?

4. Woman: I live in kind of a bad area where if I have the paper delivered, it's stolen before I can get out and get it.

   Man: That sounds pretty bad to me. I mean who would steal a newspaper.

   Woman: They just come by and pick them up even if it's just for the TV, you know.

   Question: How did the man feel when he heard that the woman's newspaper was stolen?

5. Woman: Well, I really enjoy reading the newspaper. We get the *Daily* and *Dallas Morning News*.

   Man: Do you have time to read the paper in the morning?

   Woman: Well, not in the morning. I have two children and if they go out to play or something I like to keep my eye on them. So you know I will go outside and read the paper while they are playing or sit in a chair by the window or something.

   Question: When does the woman probably read the newspaper?

6. Man: We lost the second major newspaper in Dallas within this month.

   Woman: Oh, I read that. I've been with the *Dallas Times Herald* for twenty years. Was it financial trouble that's what they went under for, wasn't it?

   Man: Yes, competition killed them and then the *Morning News* finally bought out the *Herald*.

   Question: What happened to the *Dallas Times Herald*?

Key

1. B 2. C 3. D 4. A 5. B 6. C

Notes

1. **Newsday**

   Newsday is an evening daily tabloid newspaper published in Long Island, N. Y. It was established in 1940.

2. **The New York Post**

   The New York Post is the 13th-oldest newspaper published in the United States and one of several that claim to be the oldest to have been published continually as a daily. Its editorial offices are located at 1211 Avenue of the Americas, in the New York City borough of Manhattan.

3. **The New York Daily News**

   The New York Daily News is the fifth most-widely circulated daily newspaper in the United States. The first U.S. daily printed in tabloid form, it was founded in 1919. It has won ten Pulitzer Prizes.

4. **Dallas**

   Dallas is a city in northeastern Texas, the United States. It is an important commercial, financial, and distribution center.

5. **The Dallas Times Herald**

   Founded in 1888, *The Dallas Times Herald* was once one of two major newspapers serving the Dallas, Texas (USA) area. It won three Pulitzer Prizes. On December 8, 1991, *The Dallas Morning News* bought it for $55 million and closed it the next day.

6. **The Dallas Morning News**

   The Dallas Morning News is the major daily newspaper serving the Dallas, Texas (USA) area. Today it has one of the twenty largest paid circulations in the United States. It has won numerous Pulitzers for both reporting and photography.

Longer Conversations

Conversation One

Listening Script

Directions: You will hear a conversation between two speakers. Listen to the conversation twice and answer the questions by choosing the right options.

Woman: What type of news media do you prefer for keeping up with current events?

Man: Normally I watch TV. Usually twice a day.

Woman: The news shows or like network news or national?

Man: Basically network news.

Woman: Do you like to buy newspapers?

Man: I only get the newspaper a couple of days a week. I only read it on Fridays and Sundays typically. But I get a lot of calls from *the Morning News* and *the Times Herald* where they want to sell me the paper at a special rate.

Woman: Fridays and Sundays. Why?

Man: Friday, because they have a house and garden section in the paper. For Sundays, I get the Sunday paper because of the TV schedule.

Questions:

1. What type of news media does the man prefer?
2. When does the man usually buy the newspaper?
3. Why do the Morning News and the Times Herald call the man from time to time?
4. Why does the man buy the newspaper on Sundays?

Key

1. A   2. C   3. A   4. B

Notes

1. ***Morning News***
   This refers to *the Dallas Morning News*.
2. ***Times Herald***
   This refers to *the Dallas Times Herald*.

Conversation Two

Listening Script

Directions: You will hear a conversation between two speakers. Listen to the conversation twice and write your answers to the questions in the space provided below.

Man: But isn't there something to be missed if traditional newspapers disappear?

Woman: Right.

Man: I tend to be sentimental about print — that feeling, you know. People at least my age have come to love newspapers.

Woman: You know, I'm still very sentimental about that. I like holding a newspaper. At the same time, I don't care if I'm reading it on paper, if I'm reading it online. I just want, like smart news, smart analysis, and I want to be able to read it and think about it when I want to.

Man: It seems to suggest that newspapers and magazines must look at changes in reading habits not as a death knell, but as a challenge.

Woman: I agree. The danger is that when you cling to a past, and that inhibits you from being creative enough and aggressive enough, bold enough, optimistic enough to embrace all these new opportunities.

Questions:

1. How does the man feel about the possible disappearance of newspapers?
2. According to the man, who have come to love newspapers?
3. What kind of newspapers does the woman like to read?
4. What does the woman focus on when she reads the newspapers?
5. What must traditional newspapers and magazines do today according to the man?
6. What is the danger of clinging to the past according to the woman?

Key

1. He feels very sentimental.
2. People at his age have come to love newspapers.
3. She likes to read both traditional newspapers and online ones.
4. She focuses on smart news and analysis.
5. They should regard changes in reading habits as a challenge.
6. People who do that will lose new opportunities.

Note

online newspapers

An online newspaper, also known as a web newspaper, is a newspaper that exists on the World Wide Web or the Internet. Going online created opportunities for newspapers, such as competing with broadcast journalism in presenting breaking news in a more timely manner. Online newspapers are much like hard-copy newspapers. Some newspapers have attempted to integrate the Internet into every aspect of their operations, i.e., reporters writing stories for both print and online.

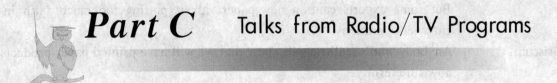

Part C   Talks from Radio/TV Programs

Purpose

This part consists of exercises based on talks excerpted from radio/TV programs. The students are expected to understand such talks and get the necessary information from them.

Detailed Plan

1. Study the new words and expressions in *Word Bank*.
2. Do the exercises based on *Excerpt One* and *Excerpt Two*.
3. Check the answers.
4. Listen to the short talks again. Pay special attention to the parts you didn't understand or misunderstood. You may refer to the script if necessary.

Excerpt One

Listening Script

Directions: You will hear a short talk from a TV program between Braver, the TV host, and Mr. Tom Griscom, the guest, about newspapers. Listen to it twice and decide whether the following statements are true (T) or false (F) according to the short talk.

Braver (host): Everyone here is well aware of predictions that printed papers are dead or dying. For one thing, rising paper prices have led some papers — like *The Wall Street Journal* — to shrink, literally. What's more, although e-readers are now just for books, companies like Plastic Logic in England are developing small wireless devices called E-paper. That will mean we won't ever have to carry real paper around to read the news. Mr. Griscom, what do you think of it?

Mr. Griscom (guest): We will progress way far ahead, no doubt about it. But I'm not ready to predict there will not be ink on paper.

Braver: There's uncertainty about the Internet, too. You haven't started making money

	off your website, yet.
Mr. Griscom:	No, we make some, but it's not going to be anywhere near what you make off a print product. Every year we'll do better, because I think what — we're understanding a little bit better of how the Internet works, how it interacts with what we are doing.
Braver:	But some experts caution newspapers about putting too much faith in their Internet operations.
Mr. Griscom:	Anybody who's realistic will know that we will have printed paper products from now till eternity.

Key

1. T 2. F 3. F 4. F 5. T

Notes

1. **there will not be ink on paper.**
   There will be no printed newspapers.
2. **It's not going to be anywhere near what you make off a print product.**
   You can earn much more money from a print product than a website.

Excerpt Two

Listening Script

Directions: You will hear a short talk from a radio program. Listen to it twice and write your answers to the questions in the space provided below.

Melissa Block, host:	A new report confirms something we've heard over and over — it is a tough time to be in the newspaper business. Figures out today show that circulation declined last year, down by more than three percent. That's some big city papers. But many small town papers are actually holding on to their audience. Some are even growing. North Country Public Radio's Brian Mann reports.
Brian Mann:	The newspaper business is, sort of, like King Kong perched on top of the Empire State Building and those little airplanes buzzing around Kong's head are the Internet and cable TV and blogs and podcasts. For 20 years, says John Sturm, president of the Newspaper Association of America, they've been chipping away at the circulation and the cultural influence of the big urban daily.
Mr. John Sturn (President, Newspaper Association of America):	There's no secret that the paid circulation of print newspapers has been declining. It's been declining for many, many years.
Mann:	But newspapers aren't one big gorilla. The industry is made up of thousands of papers from big media brands like *The Wall Street Journal*, with a total print

circulation of 1.7 million all the way down to tiny papers like *the Adirondack Daily Enterprise* in northern New York, circulation roughly 5,000.

Ms. Catherine Moore(Publisher, Daily Enterprise): Compared to the whole newspaper industry, we showed growth and circulation and online last year.

Mann: A study released this month by the Institute for World Journalism at the University of Kentucky, found that 20 million Americans still get at least some of their news from this small daily and weekly papers. One in three small town papers actually gained circulation last year. And the papers that lost circulation saw much smaller declines than urban dailies.

Questions:

1. How much did newspaper circulation decline last year?
2. How are small town newspapers doing?
3. What does Brian Mann compare the newspaper business to?
4. What have contributed to the decline of newspaper circulation?
5. What does Mr. John Sturn think of the circulation decline?
6. What is the circulation of *The Wall Street Journal* and that of the *Adirondack Daily Enterprise*?
7. How many Americans still get at least some of their news from small daily and weekly papers?

Key

1. By more than 3%.
2. They are holding on to their audience. Some are even growing.
3. King Kong on the top of the Empire State Building.
4. The Internet, cable TV, blogs and podcasts.
5. It's known to all.
6. *The Wall Street Journal* has a circulation of 1.7 million and *the Adirondack Daily Enterprise* about 5,000.
7. 20 million.

Notes

1. **King Kong**

   King Kong is a famous US film (1933) about a very large ape. In the story, King Kong captures Ann, played by Fay Wray (1907—2004), when she visits his island. She is rescued, and the ape is taken to New York to be presented as a show. He escapes and climbs to the top of the Empire State Building, where he is killed by war planes. A second version of the film was made in 1976, with Jessica Lange, and a further film, *King Kong Lives*, appeared in 1986.

2. **Adirondack Daily Enterprise**

   Adirondack Daily Enterprise is a daily newspaper in Saranac Lake, New York, USA covering general news.

   The Daily Enterprise reaches nearly 5,000 readers a day, providing news and information to the Adirondack region.

Part D Dictation

Purpose

This part contains a short talk to be dictated to the students. This exercise trains the students' skills in writing down what they have heard.

Detailed Plan

1. Study the new words and expressions in *Word Bank*.
2. Listen to the short talk from the beginning to the end without any pause.
3. Write down the sentences during the pauses when the short talk is spoken again.
4. Read the listening script and correct whatever mistakes the students may have made.
5. Listen to the short talk again if necessary.

Listening Script

Directions: You will hear a short talk about the change in people's reading habit. The short talk will be spoken twice. After you listen to it at normal speed, the short talk will be spoken again with pauses. During the pauses, write down what you hear in the space provided below.

I'm 41. I check my e-mail every morning. I look at the news from different sources, but there's just nothing like having a newspaper under your arm with a cup of coffee. And I understand you can get more information on the Internet, but just to get a general overview, I prefer the newspaper. I think it's just in human nature to resist change, and you know, most of us are used to growing up with a print publication or relying on the evening news for the sole source of our information.

Part E Fun Time

Listening Script

Directions: Listen twice to a story about a woman and her Sunday paper. Tell where the lady had been before she made the telephone call.

The irate customer, calling the newspaper offices, loudly demanded to know where her Sunday edition was.

"Ma'am," said the employee, "Today is Saturday. The Sunday paper is not delivered until Sunday."

There was quite a pause on the other end of the phone. Then, the employee heard the old lady say almost inaudibly, "So that's why no one was in church today."

Note

"So that's why no one was in church today."
Sunday is the time when people go to church. Apparently the lady had been to the church on a wrong day and didn't know why there were no people there.

Helping Others

Preview

This unit integrates various useful expressions and authentic talks about giving, needing or not needing help.

Objectives

After studying this unit, the students are expected to：
1. know the basic words and expressions about giving, needing or not needing help;
2. understand conversations and short talks about different ways to talk about helping others;
3. be able to make brief comments on helping others.

Part A Language Focus

Notes

1. **help, help out**

    The word "help" means to make it possible or easier for people to do something by doing part of their work or by giving them something they need.

    The expression "help out" usually means to help other people because they are busy or have problems.

2. **go it alone**

    It means "to start working or living on your own, especially after working or living with other people."

> *e.g. He quit working for the company and decided to go it alone as a consultant, instead.*
> *I missed the stimulation of working with others when I tried to go it alone.*

Part B   Authentic Conversations

Purpose

This part aims to familiarize the students with authentic conversations that can be heard in our daily life about helping others.

Detailed Plan

1. Study the new words and expressions in *Word Bank*.
2. Do the required exercises.
3. Check the answers.
4. Listen to the conversations again. Pay special attention to the parts you didn't understand or misunderstood. You may refer to the script if necessary.

Short Conversations

Listening Script

Directions: You will hear 6 conversations between two speakers. Listen to them and answer the following questions by choosing the right options.

1. Woman: My friend found out her boyfriend is cheating on her. I'm concerned about her. How can I help?

   Man: Be supportive. Don't force your opinion on her. Help her figure it out by talking about it. And she'll be able to work it on herself. If you're a true friend, be supportive of whatever her decision is.

   Question: What does the man suggest to the woman?

2. Woman: What's the best way to express condolences to someone whose family member has just passed away?

   Man: Avoid awkward silences. Saying "I'm sorry" can give strength because "talking is a way we can help heal." It is important not to shy away and ignore the person. Flowers, cards and charitable donations can also show support, but check with someone of the particular culture or religion for appropriate etiquette.

Question: Which of the following is not included in the man's advice?

3. Man: Giving does make us feel good. And that's probably why so many Americans do it. Experts say the best way to make your money count is to plan ahead.

Woman: Yes, you are right. But I personally think a more satisfying way to think about giving is to think about, what do I really care about? In what area would I like to make a difference?

Question: According to the woman, what is the best way to make your money count?

4. Man: I joined the Peace Corps and they sent me to Bangladesh.

Woman: Why? I mean, don't you think you've given enough?

Man: I, well, you know, I've always liked helping people.

Question: What does the woman mean?

5. Woman: I think it is our duty to love others and put others before you, and to love them like you love yourselves.

Man: Well, the reason I think giving is important is because when you give you are setting a good role model for others. Everyone should not be selfish, should be happy to give.

Question: What makes giving important according to the man?

6. Man: eBay is currently auctioning off a charity lunch with Warren Buffett. Bids started at $25,000 and last year the winning bidder paid $620,000.

Woman: $620,000 for lunch? It better be an all-you-can-eat buffet, that's all I can say.

Question: What does the woman think of the $620,000 lunch?

Key

1. B 2. C 3. D 4. B 5. C 6. C

Notes

1. Peace Corps

Established in 1961, the Peace Corps is an overseas volunteer program of the United States government. Volunteers have to be at least 18 years old and they usually sign on for a two-year term of service.

2. eBay

eBay is a popular Internet auction and shopping website managed by eBay Inc., an American Internet company. People and businesses buy and sell goods and services worldwide in eBay.com.

3. Warren Buffett

Warren Buffett is an American investor, businessman and philanthropist. He is regarded as one of the world's greatest stock market investors. In 2006, he announced a plan to give away his fortune to charity, with 83% of it going to the Bill & Melinda Gates Foundation. In 2007, he was listed among Time's 100 Most Influential People in the world.

4. an all-you-can-eat buffet

As the surname of Warren Buffett is spelt almost the same as "buffet", people often make fun of it by saying it is a buffet.

Longer Conversations

Conversation One

Listening Script

Directions: You will hear a conversation between two speakers. Listen to the conversation twice and answer the questions by choosing the right options.

Man: This holiday season, you plan to give charity gift cards to relatives and many of your friends. Is that true?

Woman: Yes. My friends already have lots of toys and games, and I want to give them something more meaningful. I think they're going to really enjoy it.

Man: Have you talked to any of them about this idea?

Woman: Yeah. They thought it was really cool.

Man: What appeals to people is that the person getting the gift card gets to choose where the money goes and both the giver and recipient can feel good about what they're doing.

Woman: Yes. Like whoever gives it to you gets the gift of giving. You get it and get the gift of giving and receiving. And the charity that you donate to gets to help people or animals or ...

Man: Many other people will do it like you. It is said that this year people are expected to spend more than $26 billion on gift cards for merchandize at retail stores and online.

Questions:

1. What is the woman going to do this holiday season?
2. Why does the woman plan to do it?
3. What do her friends and relatives think of this idea?
4. Which of the following is not true according to the conversation?

Key

1. C   2. A   3. C   4. D

Note

gift cards

A gift card is a present for friends, family and in fact anybody. Gift cards are offered by banks, shopping malls, retailers, airlines, restaurants, hotels, websites, and even state parks. With a gift card, people can buy all sorts of things ranging from furniture and home decoration through to the latest mobile phone and computer.

Conversation Two

Listening Script

Directions: You will hear a conversation between two speakers. Listen to the conversation twice and write your answers to the questions in the space provided below.

Man: Welcome back.

Woman: Thank you and Merry Christmas to you.

Man: Thank you so much. You know there are thousands and thousands of charities out there. How do you decide which one you are going to give to?

Woman: You know I always tell to people start close to home. What are some of the issues that matter to you? If you belong, for example, to a religious organization, do they have a charitable arm where they feed the poor or clothe the homeless or something like that? I mean that's where I give the bulk of my giving, but my brother had epilepsy so I gave to organizations that help the cause for epilepsy.

Man: I know that I go online now to search out all kinds of things. There must be some kind of online guide to help find charitable causes.

Woman: There really is. There's this one site that I found that I really like called GiveSpot.com. And it's a free online resource that gives you information on not just where to give but how to volunteer your time.

Questions:

1. How many charities are there according to the conversation?
2. How does the woman decide which charity she is going to give to?
3. Why did the woman give the bulk of her giving to organizations that help the cause for epilepsy?
4. What kind of website is GiveSpot.com?

Key

1. There are thousands and thousands of charities.
2. She usually starts close to home.
3. Because her brother had epilepsy.
4. It's a free online resource that gives you information on charities.

Notes

1. **charitable arm**

   A charitable arm is a branch or a part of a charity or a religious organization who gives its help to those who are in need of help.

2. GiveSpot. com

GiveSpot. com is a free volunteer and philanthropy resource center. From the site, people can quickly and easily find and evaluate more than 900,000 nonprofits and charitable organizations, locate nearly 50,000 volunteer opportunities, research more than 100,000 foundations, explore social issues and much more.

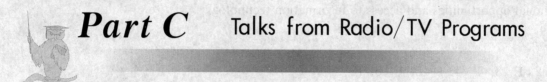

Part C Talks from Radio/TV Programs

Purpose

This part consists of exercises based on talks excerpted from radio/TV programs. The students are expected to understand such talks and get the necessary information from them.

Detailed Plan

1. Study the new words and expressions in *Word Bank*.
2. Do the exercises based on *Excerpt One* and *Excerpt Two*.
3. Check the answers.
4. Listen to the short talks again. Pay special attention to the parts you didn't understand or misunderstood. You may refer to the script if necessary.

Excerpt One

Listening Script

Directions: You will hear a short talk from a radio program about American charitable foundations. Listen to it twice and decide whether the following statements are true (T) or false (F) according to the short talk.

In the United States of America, foundations blossomed after the Civil War, when new wealth was being accumulated and there were problems to fix. Millionaire George Peabody used his and others' money to help newly-freed slaves. But it was not until the beginning of the 20th century when the first truly modern foundation was created.

A woman named Margaret Olivia Sage inherited money from her husband Russell, who was a notoriously stingy man, and she used that money for charitable purposes. The Sages were soon imitated by the Rockefellers, Henry Ford and Andrew Carnegie. Carnegie actually didn't intend to create a foundation. He had hoped to give away all his money in his lifetime, but he failed at that.

While we know of Carnegie today from his name on libraries and other institutions, another millionaire of his day has vanished from our memories. Julius Rosenwald was a merchandizing genius. In 1917, he set up a foundation to educate blacks in the south.

Today the largest operated private foundation in the world is the Bill & Melinda Gates Foundation, founded in 2000 and doubled in size by Warren Buffett in 2006. The primary aims of the foundation are globally to enhance healthcare and reduce extreme poverty, and in the United States, to expand educational opportunities and access to information technology.

Key

1. T 2. F 3. T 4. F 5. F 6. F

Notes

1. George Peabody

George Peabody, born in Massachusetts, was an entrepreneur and philanthropist who founded the Peabody Institute.

2. Margaret Olivia Sage

Margaret Olivia Sage was an American philanthropist. Upon the death of her husband she received a fortune estimated about $50,000,000. She established the Russell Sage Foundation in 1907 and donated money to Yale University, and Cornell University later.

3. Rockefellers

The Rockefeller family is an American industrial, banking, and political family of German American origin. The members of the Rockefeller family are noted for their philanthropy.

4. Andrew Carnegie

Andrew Carnegie was a Scottish-born American industrialist and philanthropist who made a fortune in the steel industry and donated millions of dollars for the benefit of the public.

5. Julius Rosenwald

Julius Rosenwald was a US manufacturer, business executive, and philanthropist. The Rosenwald Fund donated millions to support the education of African Americans and other philanthropic causes in the first half of the 20th century.

Excerpt Two

Listening Script

Directions: You will hear a short talk from a TV program. Listen to it twice and write your answers to the questions in the space provided below.

John Zarrella: They just wanted to make it easier. Three years ago these four high school girls in West Palm Beach started hanging fliers in the school hallways. Their new business, The Formal Exchange, was open. Lisa, Kramer, Sierra and Lauren had one goal in mind, to make the prom affordable for every girl and to give every girl the opportunity to be

Cinderella. Girls from any school can come in and exchange a gently worn formal dress for one that has been donated or exchanged by another girl. Every Thursday for a month during prom season, the business is open in the city library.

Unidentified female: Give me, like, a really, like, pretty that color pink necklace.

Zarrella: Nicole Harmon found the perfect dress at the perfect price.

Nicole Harmon: I think that most of these dresses are, like, over $100, and to get them for free, it's ... you can't beat that.

Zarrella: Those who don't have dresses to exchange can get one, too, just by showing proof of 10 hours community service.

Sierra McGill: Prom is kind of like part of the high school experience, so to not be able to go to something like that is really sad to hear, so to know that we're helping girls tap that opportunity is kind of rewarding.

Unidentified female: Fix me, make me look pretty.

Zarrella: The four girls, all seniors, are hoping others will step in next year and make the extra effort to carry on the business, because they say every girl should have the chance to be Cinderella.

Questions:

1. What is the name of the four girls' new business?
2. What is the goal of the new business?
3. What can girls do at The Formal Exchange if they have a formal dress?
4. How can girls get a free dress at the Formal Exchange?
5. Why does one of the four girls say it is sad to hear some girls cannot go to the prom?
6. Why do the four girls want other students to join them and carry on the business?

Key

1. The Formal Exchange.
2. To make the prom affordable for every girl.
3. They can exchange a formal dress for another.
4. By showing proof of 10 hours community service.
5. She thinks that going to the prom is part of the high school experience.
6. They believe that every girl should have the chance to be Cinderella.

Notes

1. West Palm Beach

West Palm Beach, also known as West Palm, is a city of southeast Florida opposite Palm Beach. It is a winter resort. Tourism is the basis of West Palm Beach's economy.

2. Cinderella

Cinderella is the heroine of a European folktale. More than 500 versions of the story have been recorded in Europe alone. Its essential features are a youngest daughter who is mistreated by her jealous stepmother and elder stepsisters. When the prince of the kingdom invites all the young women to a ball, Cinderella cannot go because she has only old torn clothes. Then her fairy godmother appears and magically changes six white mice into horses and a pumpkin into a carriage to take her to the ball. At the ball the Prince falls in love with her and later marries her.

3. you can't beat that

You can't get better dresses than the ones offered here without any cost. The verb "beat" in this context means "to do or be better than."

4. community service

Community service refers to services volunteered by individuals or an organization to benefit a community or its institutions.

5. Fix me

The word "fix" in this context means "make sb. look more attractive".

Part D   Dictation

Purpose

This part contains a short talk to be dictated to the students. This exercise trains the students' skills in writing down what they have heard.

Detailed Plan

1. Study the new words and expressions in *Word Bank*.
2. Listen to the short talk from the beginning to the end without any pause.
3. Write down the sentences during the pauses when the short talk is spoken again.
4. Read the listening script and correct whatever mistakes the students may have made.
5. Listen to the short talk again if necessary.

Listening Script

Directions: You will hear a short talk about the philanthropists. The short talk will be spoken twice. After you listen to it at normal speed, the short talk will be spoken again with pauses. During the pauses, write down what you hear in the space provided below.

This year, for the first time, *Forbes* has put together a list of 48 philanthropists — 4 from each of 12 countries. We aimed to identify not only some of the largest donors but also some of the most interesting — generous folks who may not make one of our rich lists but who put a large share of their money into much-needed, and sometimes unusual, projects.

Wee Lin is worth only $3.5 million, but he's opened a home for the mentally ill in Singapore and donated numerous items to North Korea. He says, "Philanthropy doesn't just mean the giving away of money. It means the giving of love. Anyone can be a philanthropist."

Note

Forbes

Forbes is an American publishing and media company. Its most important publication, *Forbes* magazine, is published bi-weekly.

Part E Fun Time

Directions: Listen twice to a story about a priest and a little boy. Tell why the boy wants to "run like hell" at the end of the story.

A priest is walking down the street one day when he notices a very small boy trying to press a doorbell on a house across the street. However, the boy is very small and the doorbell is too high for him to reach.

After watching the boy's efforts for some time, the priest steps across the street, walks up behind the little fellow and, placing his hand kindly on the child's shoulder, gives the doorbell a solid ring.

Crouching down to the child's level, the priest smiles and asks, "And now what, my little man?"

To which the boy replies, "Now we run like Hell!"

Note

"Now we run like Hell!"

Apparently the little boy is up to some mischief and the priest in fact helped him play a trick on the people living inside that house. When the people inside the house open the door, they will find no visitors outside.

Unit 13

Social Customs

Preview

This unit integrates various useful expressions and authentic talks about social customs.

Objectives

After studying this unit, the students are expected to:
1. know the basic words and expressions about social customs;
2. understand conversations and short talks about social customs;
3. be able to make brief comments on the social customs of different cultures.

Part A   Language Focus

Notes

1. taboo

Taboo is an action, object, person, or place forbidden by law or culture. Many societies believe that people who go to a taboo place or touch a taboo object will suffer serious injury. People in many parts of the world avoid taboos. For example, Australian *Aborigines*（土著人）must not say the name of a dead person aloud. Muslims must not eat pork or *shellfish*（甲壳水生动物）.

2. table manners

Table manners refer to the way one behaves when eating a meal at a table. This includes the appropriate use of utensils. Different cultures have different standards for table manners. Many table manners developed out of practicality. For example, it is generally impolite to put elbows on tables since doing so creates a risk of tipping over bowls and cups.

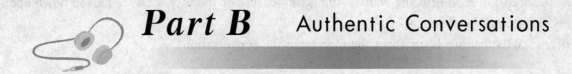

Part B Authentic Conversations

Purpose

This part aims to familiarize the students with authentic conversations that can be heard in our daily life about social customs.

Detailed Plan

1. Study the new words and expressions in *Word Bank*.
2. Do the required exercises.
3. Check the answers.
4. Listen to the conversations again. Pay special attention to the parts you didn't understand or misunderstood. You may refer to the script if necessary.

Short Conversations

Listening Script

Directions: You will hear 6 conversations between two speakers. Listen to them and answer the following questions by choosing the right options.

1. Woman: Why do girls in Sweden dress up as witches before Easter, and then go from door to door to beg for small gifts like sweets or coins?

   Man: Because Christ was still in the tomb, those are days that witches are believed to be especially active.

   Question: What do girls in Sweden look like when they go begging from door to door before Easter?

2. Woman: This is something I've never seen before. Why do these people run through the streets swinging fireballs over their heads?

   Man: The origin of the fireball ceremony is in the northeast of the country. The Vikings came here and it was an old custom for the fishermen to swing balls of fire around their heads to burn the evil spirits of the last year.

Question: What are the fireballs used for?

3. Woman: Why do you give your child an Indian name?

   Man: I want him to grow up proud of his Native American origin, unlike me, who many times felt ashamed of being Native American because of the way we were looked down upon as second-class citizens.

   Question: What can we learn about the man from the conversation?

4. Woman: Why do they announce the dawn of Easter with a 21-gun salute in Ethiopia?

   Man: When you consider that at least devout Christians have spent at least two days before Easter in total fasting, you can understand they are particularly glad to see the dawn of Easter Sunday.

   Question: Why are people in Ethiopia so glad to see the dawn of Easter Sunday?

5. Woman: Do you like the latest exhibition at the national museum?

   Man: Yes, it's about the traditional birth customs. Take your children there and they will get to learn the traditional way of carrying babies, know their family tree, understand the significance behind the food served when a baby is born.

   Question: What is the theme of the latest exhibition?

6. Man: What makes you start writing the travel tips for women?

   Woman: Well, women traveling in other countries soon find out that what is acceptable dress and behavior back home may not be in other lands. I've also found that most guide books lack information for women concerned about safety and sexual harassment.

   Question: What kind of information is not included in most guide books?

Key

1. C 2. D 3. B 4. B 5. A 6. D

Notes

1. Sweden

Sweden is a prosperous industrial nation in northern Europe. The people of Sweden have developed highly prosperous industries based on their country's three most important natural resources — timber, iron ore, and water power. The Swedish standard of living is one of the highest in the world.

2. Easter

Easter is a very important Christian festival of the year. It honors the resurrection, or the rising from the dead, of Jesus, the founder of the religion of Christianity. This religious holiday is always observed on a Sunday, but its date varies. It can fall on any Sunday between March 22 and April 25.

In many churches Easter follows a season of prayer and fasting called Lent. This is observed in memory of the 40 days Jesus is said to have fasted, or gone without food, in the desert.

3. **Christ**

   Often simply called Jesus or Christ，Jesus Christ was the man on whose ideas Christianity is based. Christians believe he was the son of God.

4. **"Because Christ was still in the tomb ..."**

   Christians believe that Jesus Christ returned to life three days after his *crucifixion*（钉死在十字架上）. So Christ was thought to be lying in the tomb between his crucifixion on *Good Friday*（耶稣受难节，即复活节前的星期五）and his resurrection on Easter Sunday.

5. **swinging fireballs**

   In the town of Stonehaven in northern Scotland，the local people celebrate what the Scots called *Hogmanay*（除夕）. They run through the streets swinging 18-pound fireballs over their heads.

6. **Viking**

   Vikings were fierce pirates and warriors who lived in Scandinavia and terrorized Europe from the late 700's to about 1100. During this period，daring Viking sailors also explored the North Atlantic Ocean and even reached America. Such deeds have given this period of European history the name the Viking Age.

7. **an Indian name**

   In this context，the word "Indian" means "native American"，i.e. of people who belong to one of the tribes who lived in North and South America before Europeans arrived.

8. **21-gun salute**

   The 21-gun salute is the highest honor that can be given by a nation. The 21-gun naval salute was first adopted by Great Britain in the 18th to 19th centuries and was later accepted as an international salute.

9. **Ethiopia**

   Ethiopia is a country in northeastern Africa. The northern part of the country，near the Red Sea，ranks among the hottest places in the world.

10. **see the dawn of Easter Sunday**

    This means that the local people who have been fasting can begin to eat because the fasting period is over.

Longer Conversations

Conversation One

Listening Script

Directions： You will hear a conversation between two speakers. Listen to it twice and decide whether the following statements are true (T) or false (F) according to the conversation.

Woman： When a woman announces herself for an appointment，should she do so using her marital status? And while we're on the subject, what do I do when I'm introduced to a lady who is of the same generation as my mother? Should I use the person's first name if the person who introduced us is doing so, or should I refer to her by her last name? If I should use the last name, what do I put in front of it, "Mrs." or "Ms."?

Man: The answer to the first question is a resounding no! It's tacky for a woman to refer to herself as "Mrs. Jane Smith," just as it would be inappropriate for a man to announce himself as "Mr. William Jones." Titles should be used by others, rather than by the person introducing or announcing himself or herself.

When meeting someone who is significantly older than you, address the person by his or her last name even if your colleague is on a first-name basis with the person. In the situation you describe, you should use "Ms." before the last name unless you're instructed to do otherwise. If the person wants you to address him or her using a first name, you will be told. Remember, you can never get into trouble for being too formal, but you can for being too informal.

Key

1. F 2. F 3. T 4. F 5. T 6. T 7. T

Note

> **even if your colleague is on a first-name basis with the person**
> even if your colleague and the person call each other by the first name

Conversation Two

Listening Script

Directions: You will hear a conversation between two speakers. Listen to the conversation twice and write your answers to the questions in the space provided below.

Elliott: Christians around the world are celebrating the resurrection of Jesus today. There are all kinds of special traditions in different cultures, some quite surprising. Folklore professor Moira Smith joins us today in our studio to tell us what's really behind those familiar eggs and bunnies.

Smith: The egg is fairly easy to explain. It's an ancient symbol for new life. And for Christians, it's a symbol of resurrection. The chick that emerges from the egg is similar to Christ emerging from the tomb.

Elliott: Oh, that sounds interesting. Then where does the Easter Bunny come from?

Smith: It began as the Easter hare in Europe. Children were encouraged — or still are encouraged, I think — to build nests for the Easter hare before Easter in the garden. And the next day on Easter Sunday, the good children would find the nest full of eggs.

Elliott: And the bad children would find it full of coal or rabbit droppings.

Smith: That's right. And then in the 19th century in America, we developed the Easter Bunny out of the European Easter hare, and we changed it somewhat from having the hare who lays eggs to a bunny that simply brings eggs. And hares — there's a lot of folklore about hares. They're symbols of fertility. They're also symbols of sexual attraction.

Questions:

1. Why is the egg a symbol of resurrection for Christians?
2. What are children encouraged to do before Easter in Europe?
3. What would bad children find in their nest on Easter Sunday?
4. What did the European Easter hare change into in America?
5. What does the hare stand for?

Key

1. Because the chick that emerges from the egg is similar to Christ emerging from the tomb.
2. To build nests for the Easter hare in the garden.
3. Coal or rabbit droppings.
4. The Easter bunny that brings eggs.
5. Fertility and sexual attraction.

Notes

1. **Easter egg**

   Easter eggs are specially decorated eggs given out to celebrate the Easter holiday or springtime. Christians adopted the egg as an Easter symbol because of the relationship between Easter and the renewal of life. The oldest tradition is to use dyed and painted chicken eggs. These are often hidden, supposedly by the Easter Bunny, for children to find on Easter morning.

2. **Easter Bunny**

   The Easter Bunny is a symbol of Easter. According to tradition the Easter Bunny makes his visit every year, scattering brightly-colored eggs as he goes. In ancient times the rabbit was a symbol of fertility, associated with springtime and renewal of life.

Part C   Talks from TV Programs

Purpose

This part consists of exercises based on talks excerpted from TV programs. The students are expected to understand such talks and get the necessary information from them.

Detailed Plan

1. Study the new words and expressions in *Word Bank*.
2. Do the exercises based on *Excerpt One* and *Excerpt Two*.
3. Check the answers.
4. Listen to the short talks again. Pay special attention to the parts you didn't understand or misunderstood. You may refer to the script if necessary.

Excerpt One

Listening Script

Directions: You will hear a short talk from a TV program. Listen to it twice and decide whether the following statements are true (T) or false (F) according to the short talk.

In Ghana the xylophone is played by local people in the northwest region. This African musical instrument is made from dried root and cords, and produces unique sounds. Xylophone music is usually played during festivals, funerals, and other special locations.

There is a myth that a man threatened to kill a fairy who was playing the xylophone in the forest if she did not show him all the secrets of building it and playing the instrument. After being taught, the man killed the fairy anyway, roasted her and ate her with his friends.

The famous myth has remained part of the history of the instrument, so it was believed that women who played it would probably have problems getting a husband. This traditional belief, which has been with the people from old times, has caused great fear among women in the region and in the end has oppressed their artistic talent.

Key

1. F 2. T 3. F 4. T 5. F

Notes

1. **Ghana**

   Ghana is a tropical country in western Africa, lying on the Gulf of Guinea. Most of the people of Ghana are black Africans. Cacao seeds, which are used to make chocolate, are the country's most important crop and its leading export. Ghana gained its independence in 1957 from British rule and is a member of the *Commonwealth of Nations*(英联邦).

2. **xylophone**

   The xylophone is a percussion instrument that consists chiefly of a set of wooden bars arranged on a frame like the keys of a piano. A musician strikes the instrument's bars with a *mallet*(木槌) to produce a hard, brittle sound. It is found in the folk music of many cultures and has long been one of the principal instruments of African music. Its origins are unclear.

Excerpt Two

Listening Script

Directions: You will hear a short talk from a TV program. Listen to it twice and answer the questions by choosing the right options.

Cooper:	A mother and father point to their daughter's wedding picture. This marriage, they say, cost her, her life. Their daughter Margon committed suicide, trapped in a marriage she felt she couldn't leave, trapped by a culture in which some women are killed for wanting a divorce.
Unidentified Female:	She and her sister always talked about life. She told her sister she didn't like her mother-in-law. When I went to see her after the wedding, she was upset. I asked her how she was doing, but she said she was OK. We wanted to take her back from her husband. But then we learned she died.
Cooper:	In Turkey's poor conservative southeast, if a woman is accused of shaming her husband's family by asking for divorce, committing adultery, or even being raped, she risks being murdered. It's called an honor killing, a centuries-old tradition designed to restore a family's honor.
	Today, some women are still being killed or pressured into committing suicide. And, in June, the United Nations sent a special envoy to investigate. The U. N. concluded that, while many of the deaths were suicides, some were honor killings disguised as a suicide or an accident.
	Turkey has recently changed its laws, mandating life sentences for men convicted of honor killings. But traditions die hard, and many men here still believe honor killings are justified.
Unidentified Male:	We are bound by the rules. If a woman runs away, she must be killed.

Questions:

1. Why was the old couple's daughter killed?
2. What did the old couple want to do when they learned that their daughter was unhappy at her husband's home?
3. Why do people in some areas of Turkey practice the so-called honor killing?
4. What is the conclusion made by the U. N. envoy about honor killing in Turkey?
5. What do many men think of honor killing in some parts of Turkey?

Key

1. C   2. A   3. B   4. B   5. A

Notes

1. **Turkey's poor conservative southeast**

   The Republic of Turkey lies partly in Asia and partly in Europe. Peoples and ideas from both regions have shaped the country's history and culture.

   The country has a north-south extent that ranges from about 300 to 400 miles (480 to 640 km), and it stretches about 1,000 miles from west to east. Turkey is bounded on the north by the Black Sea, on the northeast by Georgia and Armenia, on the east by Azerbaijan and Iran, on the southeast by Iraq and Syria, on the southwest and west by the Mediterranean Sea and the Aegean Sea, and on the northwest by Greece and Bulgaria.

2. **honor killing**

   An honor killing is the murder of a victim by male family members against female family members, who are held to have brought dishonor upon the family. The practice is most common in countries of the Middle East.

   A woman can be targeted by her family for a variety of reasons, including: refusing to enter into an arranged marriage, being the victim of a sexual assault, seeking a divorce or committing adultery.

Part D Dictation

Purpose

This part contains a short talk to be dictated to the students. This exercise trains the students' skills in writing down what they have heard.

Detailed Plan

1. Study the new words and expressions in *Word Bank*.
2. Listen to the short talk from the beginning to the end without any pause.
3. Write down the sentences during the pauses when the short talk is spoken again.
4. Read the listening script and correct whatever mistakes the students may have made.
5. Listen to the short talk again if necessary.

Listening Script

Directions: You will hear a short talk about social customs. The short talk will be spoken twice. After you listen to it at normal speed, the short talk will be spoken again with pauses. During the pauses, write down what you hear in the space provided below.

大学英语自主听力指南4

Social customs are part of the culture shared by members of a social group. Like all cultural traits, customs are a form of learned behavior and differ among different peoples. For example, eating is a biological requirement for all people, but table manners and customs of food preparation vary among social groups. In isolated communities, most customs remain unchanged from generation to generation. The majority of people in such societies believe the old ways are the best. In modern industrial societies, however, customs change more easily. A number of factors, including new inventions and contact with other cultures, may lead to such changes.

Part E Fun Time

Listening Script

Directions: Listen twice to a humorous story about a disappointed salesman of Coca Cola. Retell the story to your classmates and explain why he was not successful with his Middle East assignment.

The disappointed salesman of Coca Cola returns from his Middle East assignment. A friend asked, "Why weren't you successful with the Arabs?"

The salesman explained, "When I got posted in the Middle East, I was very confident that I will make a good sales pitch as Cola is unknown there. But, I had a problem. I don't speak Arabic. So, I planned to convey the message through 3 posters. First poster, a man crawling through the hot desert sand, totally exhausted. Second, the man is drinking our Cola. And third, our man is now totally refreshed. Then these posters were pasted all over the place."

"That should have worked", said the friend.

He replied, "Well, I didn't know Arabic, neither did I realize that Arabs read from right to left ..."

Notes

1. **Coca Cola**

   The soft drink Coca-Cola was invented by the Atlanta pharmacist John S. Pemberton in 1886. It was sold in more than 200 countries and dominated the world soft drink market throughout the 20th century. Its name derived from its two principal drug ingredients, the Peruvian coca leaf and the West African kola nut.

2. **"... neither did I realize that Arabs read from right to left ..."**

   Both Arabic and Hebrew, and the languages using the Arabic or the Hebrew alphabet, such as Persian and Yiddish, are written from right to left (except for their numbers).

Unit 14

Making Complaints

Preview

This unit integrates various useful expressions and authentic talks about making and responding to complaints.

Objectives

After studying this unit, the students are expected to:

1. know the basic words and expressions about making or responding to complaints;
2. understand conversations and short talks related to complaints;
3. be able to make or respond to complaints.

Part A   Language Focus

Notes

1. **complain, grumble, moan, whinge, whine**

   "Complain" is the general word people use to say that they are annoyed, unhappy or not satisfied about sb./sth.

   e.g. If the hotel isn't satisfactory, you should complain to the Tourist Office.

   The word "grumble" means to keep complaining in bad-tempered or unhappy way.

   "Moan" is an informal word. It means to make a complaint in an unhappy voice, usually about something which does not seem important to other people.

"Whinge" is a British word, meaning to keep complaining in an annoying way.

"Whine" means to complain in an annoying, crying voice.

Of these four words "grumble, moan, whinge, whine", "grumble" tells you how the person who is complaining feels (= the complainer in a bad mood); the other three tell you more about how the people listening to the complaints feel (= the complaining is annoying them).

2. go on at sb. about sth.

It means to continue to criticize someone or ask them to do something in an annoying way.

e.g. My father is always going on at me about my performance at school.

3. turn a deaf ear

It means to be unwilling to listen to what someone is saying or asking.

e.g. The factory owners turned a deaf ear to the demands of the workers.

When I tell him to stop drinking, he turns a deaf ear to me.

Part B Authentic Conversations

Purpose

This part aims to familiarize the students with authentic conversations that can be heard in our daily life about helping others.

Detailed Plan

1. Study the new words and expressions in *Word Bank*.
2. Do the required exercises.
3. Check the answers.
4. Listen to the conversations again. Pay special attention to the parts you didn't understand or misunderstood. You may refer to the script if necessary.

Short Conversations

Listening Script

Directions: You will hear 6 conversations between two speakers. Listen to them and answer the following questions by choosing the right options.

1. Woman: Yes, I'm disappointed, but you know what? Getting in the National Championship Game

two years in a row was a feat in itself, but too bad we lost.

Man: But it was an exciting, competitive season, not just for your team but for all of college football.

Question: Why does the woman feel disappointed?

2. Man: What do you think of this clinic? It's the only one in our small town.

Woman: It's better than I expected, but the sources that have been provided, I mean, they are not up to standard. I've been in the clinic inside. They have only one doctor today, and only 30 patients that will be attended to. I mean, it's not acceptable.

Question: What does the woman think of the clinic?

3. Woman: Now, you're telling me the cheaper the shoes, the higher the tariff and someone with comfortable position is spending $300 to $400 on a pair of shoes, is paying literally nothing on the tariff tax coming in?

Man: You're getting mad. I can see it.

Woman: Yes, I am. I'm a little bit upset because I work very hard for my little pennies and I have to put up with a lot of nonsense at work.

Man: Nobody set out to tax the poor more than the rich. It happened by accident.

Question: What are the speakers talking about?

4. Man: Why are you always so critical about advertising? After all, those ads help pay your salary.

Woman: Yes, advertising revenue does support the fine journalists at this and many other establishments in all sorts of media. But there's nothing that says ads that support our livelihoods have to be bad.

Question: What does the woman mean?

5. Man: I don't like the music that they play over and over again without really necessarily quality.

Woman: Ah that's the complaint I make to my husband about the radio station too. They are playing one of their ten songs. It seems like every week they pick ten and they just play them over and over.

Question: What is the woman complaining about?

6. Man: Most small business owners have to deal with unhappy customers, including some that bad-mouth the business. Did this situation go farther than that?

Woman: Yes. Unfortunately this turned into a kind of extreme situation. The customer took his complaints public by making up leaflets complaining about the company, posting them around the neighborhood, and then posting a website about his complaints. It comes up very high in the search results when you Google this company.

Question: Which of the following is not mentioned in the dialogue about the customer making his complaints in an extreme situation?

Key

1. A   2. C   3. B   4. C   5. D   6. D

Note

> **tariff**
>
> A tariff is a tax imposed by a government on imported or in some countries exported goods.

Longer Conversations

Conversation One

Listening Script

Directions: You will hear a conversation between two speakers. Listen to the conversation twice and answer the questions by choosing the right options.

Man: All right. So here is my bottom-line question. If you're so good at complaining, what's the best thing you ever got by complaining?

Woman: I actually got a totally new car, replacement car, for a car that had 30,000 miles.

Man: That's impressive. How did you do it?

Woman: This car just kept using oil and oil and oil, and I complained and complained. And this complaint was two years. Eventually I spoke to a guy and said, you know, "I need a new car". And he said, "I can't give you a new car. It's too old." I said, "But it wasn't too old when I started complaining." So we battled on and battled on. Eventually they got so fed up with me and they gave me a brand new car. So that was my triumph.

Man: A whole new car?

Woman: Yes, whole new car.

Man: That's amazing.

Questions:

1. How many miles did the woman's old car have?
2. Why did the woman complain about her car?
3. Why did the auto company give a whole new car to the woman eventually?

Key

1. B   2. D   3. C

Conversation Two

Listening Script

Directions: You will hear a conversation between two speakers. Listen to the conversation twice and write your answers to the questions in the space provided below.

Man: Vera, good morning to you.

Woman: Good morning, Meredith.

Man: First impulse when you're angry is to shout, but you say that's the wrong way to start.

Woman: That is the wrong way to start. You've got to be calm, cool and collected. If you're angry, if you're lashing out, that's only going to make the bad situation worse and probably make it more difficult to resolve the issue.

Man: And also polite, you say.

Woman: Very polite. You also want to act quickly if it's something you can resolve right then and there on the spot in the store with the store manager or someone else in authority, go ahead and do it there. If not, then you want to appeal to the company's consumer affairs office or take it even higher than that. You could even call a local reporter, TV stations, the newspapers, whatever it takes to actually get the word out there because sometimes they love those consumer pieces.

Questions:

1. According to the man, what do people usually do at the moment when they are angry?
2. Why does the woman think that shouting is a wrong way to start?
3. What should people do when they're angry according to the woman?
4. What does the woman suggest to resolve the issue?

Key

1. Shout.
2. Because it will only make the situation worse and make it more difficult to resolve the issue.
3. They should be calm, cool, collected, and polite.
4. Talk with the store manager or someone in authority, appeal to the company's consumer affairs office or call mass media.

Note

> **the company's consumer affairs office**
>
> The consumer affairs office deals with consumers' complaints and is supposed to protect consumers' interests. Generally, consumers have the following rights under consumer protection laws: (1) Right to safety: protection from hazardous goods. (2) Right to be informed: availability of information required for weighing alternatives, and protection from false and misleading claims in advertising and labeling practices. (3) Right to choose: availability of competing goods and services that offer alternatives in terms of price, quality, service. (4) Right to be heard.

Part C   Talks from TV Programs

Purpose

This part consists of exercises based on talks excerpted from TV programs. The students are expected to understand such talks and get the necessary information from them.

Detailed Plan

1. Study the new words and expressions in *Word Bank*.
2. Do the exercises based on *Excerpt One* and *Excerpt Two*.
3. Check the answers.
4. Listen to the short talks again. Pay special attention to the parts you didn't understand or misunderstood. You may refer to the script if necessary.

Excerpt One

Listening Script

Directions: You will hear a short talk from a TV program about making complaints. Listen to it twice and decide whether the following statements are true (T) or false (F) according to the short talk.

Rain：   Good morning, Susan.

Susan： Good morning.

Rain：   So where do people go wrong when they complain?

Susan： You know, people don't know how to do it effectively. They don't do it right all the time. You know, I have seen a complaint letter that is 10 pages long. I actually saw a letter somebody wrote to a company that was written in pencil on the back of a piece of wall paper. Hey, that's not going to get you help. It's really not.

Rain：   So what is the right way?

Susan： I always suggest that people write a letter first to a company, if you have a problem. Now, don't write the 10-page letter. It should be one page only. Don't write it in pencil. Type it out. In the first paragraph, you need to state the problem and then give a brief history. Then you need to ask for specific action. State how you can be reached and make sure you include your phone number, your address, and your e-mail.

Rain：   Have you ever written any complaint letter?

Susan: Oh, I write letters all the time. I once went to a movie and the lighting was all wrong. They didn't dim the lights in the movie, so it ruined my experience. I wrote a letter to the movie theater, I got two free tickets.

Rain: You said something interesting. Thank you.

Key

1. F 2. T 3. F 4. T 5. F 6. T

Excerpt Two

Listening Script

Directions: You will hear a short talk from a TV program. Listen to it twice and answer the questions by choosing the right options.

Colmes: The owner of the world-famous Geno's Cheesesteaks in Philadelphia has come under fire recently for posting a sign that reads, "This is America. When ordering, please speak English" at his restaurant's cash register.

The city's Commission on Human Relations has filed a complaint against Geno's, citing violations of the city's anti-discrimination laws.

Joining us now, radio talk show host Michael Smerconish.

Michael, welcome to our show.

Smerconish: Thank you, Alan.

Colmes: I think we probably agree on this, they certainly should have a right — and by the way, the ACLU agrees, too. They should have the right to put that sign up there. And I think Pat's Steaks down the street ought to just say all languages spoken here. Right?

Smerconish: Well, I agree. If what you're arguing is that the market ought to sort this out …

Colmes: Absolutely.

Smerconish: … instead of government intervention, I'm all for that.

I mean, if you come to Philly, you know this. You go to Ninth and Passyunk. You either go to Geno's on the north side or Pat's on the south side. Joe Vento, Geno's, has staked out this territory. And if you don't like it, vote with your feet.

And I think that the mistake here is the Pennsylvania Human Relations Commission is asserting a claim for discrimination. They're barking up the wrong tree, and they're going to lose. And that will be a setback for prosecuting real cases of discrimination.

Questions:

1. What does the city's Commission on Human Relations think of Geno's sign?
2. What does Colmes, the TV program host, think of the sign?
3. What's Michael Smerconish's suggestion to those people who want to have steaks in the city?
4. What does Smerconish mean by Ninth and Passyunk?
5. What is Smerconish's opinion about the government's complaint?

Key

1. B 2. A 3. C 4. A 5. C

Notes

1. **Geno's Cheesesteaks**

   Geno's Steaks is a Philadelphia restaurant specializing in cheesesteaks, a sandwich principally of thinly sliced pieces of steak and melted cheese on a long roll. It was founded in 1966 by Joe Vento.

2. **Philadelphia**

   The largest city in Pennsylvania, located in the southeastern part of the state on the Delaware river.

3. **Commission on Human Relations**

   Established in 1951, the Philadelphia Commission on Human Relations (PCHR) is the City agency that enforces civil rights laws and deals with all matters of inter-group conflict within the city.

4. **ACLU**

   ACLU is short for the American Civil Liberties Union. It is a nonprofit legal organization founded in 1920 by Roger Baldwin. Its goal is to use law and courts to protect civil and constitutional freedoms of US citizens.

5. **Pat's Steaks**

   Pat's King of Steaks (also known as Pat's Steaks) is a Philadelphia restaurant located at the intersection of 9th Street and Passyunk Avenue in south Philadelphia.

6. **Philly**

   Philly is short for Philadelphia.

7. **Ninth and Passyunk**

   Ninth and Passyunk refer to Ninth Street and Passyunk Avenue respectively. They go across each other.

8. **They're barking up the wrong tree**

   "Bark up the wrong tree" is an idiom which means to attempt or pursue the wrong thing, to misdirect one's efforts, etc.

   e.g. The police spent three months barking up the wrong tree on the murder investigation.

Part D   Dictation

Purpose

This part contains a short talk to be dictated to the students. This exercise trains the students' skills in writing down what they have heard.

Detailed Plan

1. Study the new words and expressions in *Word Bank*.
2. Listen to the short talk from the beginning to the end without any pause.
3. Write down the sentences during the pauses when the short talk is spoken again.
4. Read the listening script and correct whatever mistakes the students may have made.
5. Listen to the short talk again if necessary.

Listening Script

Directions: You will hear a short talk about complaining. The short talk will be spoken twice. After you listen to it at normal speed, the short talk will be spoken again with pauses. During the pauses, write down what you hear in the space provided below.

I'm sure you've heard the old saw: Nobody likes a complainer. It's probably also true that very few people actually like complaining.

Like it or not, though, sometimes complaining is a necessity, but there are a couple of questions you have to ask yourself before you step down that path. Are you doing it to get something off your chest or to fix a problem, get some sort of action in response? If something is not put right, how far do you intend to go?

Some business owners take complaints very seriously, kill the complainer with kindness, offer apologies and recompense, and want the complaint taken care of with speed and thoroughness. Other businesses see the complainer as an irritant to be ignored, as someone whose future business has probably been lost anyway, so why expend so much energy addressing a problem.

Part E   Fun Time

Listening Script

Directions: Listen to the song *Down by the Salley Gardens* and try to appreciate the beauty of the lyrics as well as the music.

Down by the Salley Gardens

Down by the salley gardens my love and I did meet;
She passed the salley gardens with little snow-white feet.
She bid me take love easy, as the leaves grow on the tree;
But I, being young and foolish, with her would not agree.

In a field by the river my love and I did stand,

And on my leaning shoulder she laid her snow-white hand.

She bid me take life easy, as the grass grows on the weirs;

But I was young and foolish, and now am full of tears.

Note

Down by the Salley Gardens

    Down by the Salley Gardens is a relatively recent Irish folk song. Its text is derived from a well-known poem included in William Butler Yeats' poetry collection published in 1889. The famous Irish poet W. B. Yeats (1865—1939) won the 1923 Nobel Prize for literature.

Emergency

Preview

This unit integrates various useful expressions and authentic talks about emergency.

Objectives

After studying this unit, the students are expected to:

1. know the basic words and expressions related to emergency;
2. understand conversations and short talks about emergency;
3. be able to seek emergency help in English and talk about emergencies.

Part A   Language Focus

Notes

1. **red alert**

   Red alert is a warning or alarm that indicates a situation of the highest priority or greatest urgency. In the US, the warning scale consists of five color-coded threat levels. They are:

   Red: severe risk

   Orange: high risk

   Yellow: significant risk

   Blue: general risk

   Green: low risk

2. fire engine

It is a special large vehicle that carries equipment and the people that stop fires burning.

Part B Authentic Conversations

Purpose

This part aims to familiarize the students with authentic conversations that can be heard in our daily life about emergency.

Detailed Plan

1. Study the new words and expressions in *Word Bank*.
2. Do the required exercises.
3. Check the answers.
4. Listen to the conversations again. Pay special attention to the parts you didn't understand or misunderstood. You may refer to the script if necessary.

Short Conversations

Listening Script

Directions: You will hear 6 conversations between two speakers. Listen to them and answer the following questions by choosing the right options.

1. Man: One good reason for saving money obviously is because life is, in fact, unpredictable. You never know when or where you're going to need that nest egg to get out of a tight spot.

   Woman: Yeah. Emergencies always come up. That's why they're called emergencies and they always have a price tag attached to them.

   Question: Why do people save money according to the man?

2. Woman: Do you think Canadians, on the whole, are prepared in the event of an emergency?

   Man: Not quite. I think we are becoming more and more aware as we experience lessons learned. And of course we can't ever believe that we're going to be impacted by either a weather-caused emergency or some other event. So I think preparedness is very, very important.

   Question: What does the man think is important in the event of an emergency?

3. Man: Nine-one-one, what's the nature of your emergency?

   Woman: This is Mount Hood. We have seven people down.

   Man: What's the location of your emergency?

   Woman: This is on Mount Hood on the south side, about 800 feet from the peak. We have seven people down, possibly four injured. They fell into the crevasse.

   Question: How many people need medical help in the emergency?

4. Woman: In a car accident, if you bleed internally only a small amount, you maybe feel fine for a few hours to a few days to even up to a few weeks afterwards.

   Man: That is the fear. Pumped with adrenaline, victims sometimes walk away from the accident not knowing about the grave danger they are in.

   Question: Which of the following is true according to the conversation?

5. Man: This is AA flight 489. We need to declare an emergency. We got a low fuel situation. We're not sure if it's a fuel leak or what, but we need to get on the ground right away, please. We'd like to land on 17 center please.

   Woman: Okay, sir. We will tell approach control your request. I am sure they will try and accommodate you.

   Question: Why does the man declare an emergency?

6. Man: Talking about camping in the forest, what should we do if we meet a bear?

   Woman: Should you meet a bear, don't run away. The bear can run faster. Instead, stay calm and do not make any sudden moves.

   Question: What should we do if we meet a bear in the forest?

Key

1. A   2. C   3. A   4. A   5. B   6. B

Notes

1. **nest egg**

   It refers to a sum of money that you have saved so that you can use it in the future.

   e.g. They had to use part of their retirement nest egg to pay for their son's college fees.

   They have a little nest egg tucked away somewhere for a rainy day.

2. **tight spot**

   It means a difficult situation.

   e.g. I hope you can help get me out of a tight spot.

3. **Nine-one-one**

   It is the telephone number used in the US to call the emergency services.

4. **Mount Hood**

   This is a mountain peak in northern Oregon of the US. It rises to 3,426 meters above sea level and is the highest point in Oregon. Mount Hood is a recreational center, attracting skiers and mountain climbers.

5. AA flight 489

This refers to Flight No. 489 of the American Airlines, one of the largest airlines in the world. It serves some 250 destinations in about 40 countries in the Americas, Europe, and the Asia-Pacific region.

6. approach control

It is a radio guidance service for aircraft within 10 to 20 miles (16 to 32 kilometers) of their destination airport.

Longer Conversations

Conversation One

Listening Script

Directions: You will hear a conversation between two speakers. Listen to the conversation twice and answer the questions by choosing the right options.

Man: In general, in any type of medical emergency, what's your best advice?

Woman: First, keep calm. Get your priorities straight. And make sure that the person is breathing and has a good pulse. It's important to know how to take a pulse. It's important to know how to assess an emergency, because they happen in front of regular folks. Emergencies do not happen in front of doctors. They happen at home, on the street. We have to know what to do.

Man: OK. Let's talk about what you should do if someone is having a heart attack. You say the things to do include: lay the person down, then check their pulse. Then call 911.

Woman: Right.

Man: And if the person does not have a pulse, perform CPR.

Woman: But you first call 911, because their arrival is actually the most critical factor. But we all need to know how to do CPR.

Man: And if you don't, can the 911 person talk you through it?

Woman: They can talk you through it. They're very good at that. They're very calming. They have a protocol on how they will ask you questions and ascertain the extent of the emergency.

Questions:

1. What are the speakers discussing in the conversation?
2. Which of the following is not mentioned when the two speakers talk about what to do with someone suffering a heart attack?
3. When someone has a heart attack, what is the most important thing to do to save the person's life?
4. From whom can you seek help if you don't know how to do CPR?

Key

1. B 2. D 3. B 4. A

Note

> **CPR**
>
> CPR stands for cardiopulmonary resuscitation. It is a life-saving procedure that includes the timed external compression of the *anterior*（身体前部的）chest wall to stimulate blood flow by pumping the heart, alternating with mouth to mouth breathing to provide oxygen.

Conversation Two

Listening Script

Directions: You will hear a conversation between two speakers. Listen to the conversation twice and answer the questions by choosing the right options.

Woman: How young do kids, well, let's say how old do kids have to be to understand how to call 911? When do you start talking to your children?

Man: Well, it's never too early, of course. But as early as three or four years of age, of course, they can start to understand how to manipulate the telephone and the issues involved.

Woman: Now once you've determined that it's time to talk to your child, what's the first thing that you need to do? How do you begin the conversation?

Man: Well, explain how they can help family member or somebody else or help themselves. And then you explain to them what 911 will do for them. Then you explain how to physically manipulate the equipment, the telephone.

Woman: Do they need to know their own home address or can that be traced?

Man: Well, most of the 911 installations throughout the country do have what we call E-911 where we do get the address, but you still want to emphasize to the children to stay on the line with the operator and always make sure that they provide the address. Because sometimes there could be an equipment failure or some other reason, even though we do get it 99 percent of the time.

Woman: OK, Sean, thank you. Thank you very much.

Questions:

1. When can kids start to understand how to call 911?
2. After explaining what 911 is all about, what should parents teach their kids to do?
3. Why do kids need to know their own home address?

Key

1. A   2. B   3. D

Note

> **E-911**
>
> E-911, i.e. Enhanced 911, refers to 911 emergency service *on mobile*（移动的）and Internet telephone calls.

Part C   Talks from Radio/TV Programs

Purpose

This part consists of exercises based on talks excerpted from Radio/TV programs. The students are expected to understand such talks and get the necessary information from them.

Detailed Plan

1. Study the new words and expressions in *Word Bank*.
2. Do the exercises based on *Excerpt One* and *Excerpt Two*.
3. Check the answers.
4. Listen to the short talks again. Pay special attention to the parts you didn't understand or misunderstood. You may refer to the script if necessary.

Excerpt One

Listening Script

Directions: You will hear a short talk from a radio program. Listen to it twice and answer the questions by choosing the right options.

Growing up during the golden age of disaster movies, my sister and I were acutely aware of all the things that could go wrong around us. Films like *Jaws* and *Earthquake* and *The Towering Inferno* showed us how one tragic event could trigger other tragedies until escape was futile. We knew that having a plan was important. So we designed strategies for dealing with every possible situation, from natural disasters to nuclear war to unlikely crime scenarios.

In case of tornado, we decided that we'd grab the pets and as many cans as we could carry, and hide in the basement. If there was a nuclear attack, we'd seal all the windows with aluminum foil and shower every two hours. In case of a flood, we'd inflate the little raft in the garage and haul it up to the roof so we'd be safe until the water rose very high. As unrealistic as some of our approaches might have seemed even then, we knew that to navigate a world in which flood washed away cities and villages, planes crashed and the earth stared open, swallowing cars whole, we would have to be well prepared.

Questions:

1. What did the author and her sister do to cope with every possible disaster?

2. Which of the following disasters is not mentioned in their plan?

3. What can be inferred about the speaker and her sister from the passage?

Key

1. B   2. C   3. D

Notes

1. *Jaws*

   Jaws is the title of a horror film directed by Steven Spielberg in 1975. It is based on Peter Benchley's best-selling novel.

2. *Earthquake*

   Earthquake is the title of a disaster film directed by Mark Robson in 1974. Its plot concerns the struggle for survival after a catastrophic earthquake destroys the city of Los Angeles, California.

3. *The Towering Inferno*

   The Towering Inferno is the title of a disaster film directed by John Guillermin in 1974. The film was adapted by Stirling Silliphant from the novels *The Tower* by Richard Martin Stern and *The Glass Inferno* by Thomas N. Scortia and Frank M. Robinson.

Excerpt Two

Listening Script

Directions: You will hear a short talk from a TV program. Listen to it twice and answer the questions by choosing the right options.

Reporter:	At the height of the evening rush, a massive underground explosion sent a geyser of steam, water and debris shooting into the air.
Unidentified Male:	Where this vast explosion, the building shook a little bit and small particles of rocks came to our window on the 27th floor.
Reporter:	It happened near Grand Central Terminal in the heart of Midtown Manhattan. A steam pipe installed back in 1924 burst. The explosion erupted like a volcano out of the ground. It tore a huge hole in the street and sent people running for their lives.
Unidentified Male:	Certainly people panicked a little bit and was crying, shouting, because obviously everybody thinks of 9/11, you know, a repeat of this.
Unidentified Female:	The whole street was chaos. People were running. Their shoes were falling off. They were pushing each other and pulling each other. And we looked up and there was smoke billowing out of this building.
Reporter:	New York mayor Michael Bloomberg rushed to reassure the public.
Mayor Michael Bloomberg:	There is no reason to believe that there was any terrorism involved whatsoever. It is probably just a failure of the part of our infrastructure.
Reporter:	Bloomberg said one person died of a heart attack. Two dozen others were

injured. The immediate concern for city officials and those who live and work in the area was what was in the material shooting out of the ground.

Jessica Leighton, NYC Dept. of Health and Mental Hygiene: People who are in the buildings in the areas, close their windows, that they — If there's air-conditioning in the building, that they turn it on to recirculate, that people stay off the area — stay out of the area. If people were exposed to any debris, they should wash with soap and water, they should remove their clothes and put them in a plastic bag.

Questions:

1. What happened at the height of the evening rush?
2. How did people react to the accident?
3. Which of the following is not true on the street after the accident?
4. Who is Michael Bloomberg?
5. What are people advised to do after the accident?

Key

1. B   2. D   3. D   4. C   5. A

Notes

1. **Grand Central Terminal**

   Grand Central Terminal is a terminal station in Midtown Manhattan in New York City. Constructed in 1903 to 1913, it is the largest train station in the world by number of platforms with 67 train tracks on two different levels.

2. **Midtown Manhattan**

   Midtown, along with "Uptown" and "Downtown," is one of the three major subdivisions of Manhattan, New York City. It's home to some world-famous commercial buildings such as Rockefeller Center, Radio City Music Hall, and the Empire State Building.

3. **Michael Bloomberg**

   Michael Rubens Bloomberg (born February 14, 1942) is an American businessman and the Mayor of New York City.

Part D   Dictation

Purpose

This part contains a short talk to be dictated to the students. This exercise trains the students' skills in writing down what they have heard.

Detailed Plan

1. Study the new words and expressions in *Word Bank*.
2. Listen to the short talk from the beginning to the end without any pause.
3. Write down the sentences during the pauses when the short talk is spoken again.
4. Read the listening script and correct whatever mistakes the students may have made.
5. Listen to the short talk again if necessary.

Listening Script

Directions: Listen to a short talk twice. When you listen to it the first time, you should listen carefully for its general idea. When you listen to it the second time, you are required to fill in the blanks numbered from 1 to 8 with the exact words you have just heard. For blanks numbered from 9 to 11 you are required to fill the missing information with the exact words you have just heard or write down the main points in your own words.

When we were young, our emergency plans were not always entirely logical. In case our house <u>caught</u> on fire, for example, I was <u>supposed</u> to grab my bear and the dog, <u>stuff</u> them in a pillow and throw them out the window. My sister was in <u>charge</u> of the cat. Next, we'd throw one of our mattresses out the window and then jump out the window, <u>landing</u>, of course, in the middle of the mattress. Not the soundest plan, <u>considering</u> that there was a perfectly good fire escape ladder in the <u>hall</u> closet, but we had never used that ladder. We weren't sure how to use it. And the picture on the box made us <u>nervous</u>.

Sadly, <u>we didn't run our escape plan by my mom</u>, who might have liked to know that if there was a fire, her two daughters would die struggling to shove a mattress out the window. But it seemed more comforting to have a plan that our parents weren't in on. After all, most adults seemed <u>to be in serious denial when it came to disasters</u>. When you tried to discuss with them the possibility that, say, a comet might fall on the house, <u>they didn't have any clue how they would handle it</u>.

Key

1. caught 2. supposed 3. stuff 4. charge 5. landing 6. considering 7. hall 8. nervous
9. we didn't run our escape plan by my mom
10. to be in serious denial when it came to disasters
11. they didn't have any clue how they would handle it

Part E Fun Time

Listening Script

Directions: Listening to a humorous story about a dead dog and a sniffing cat twice. Discuss with your classmates and tell what makes the lady have a fit at the end of the story.

A lady rushes into the veterinarian and screams, "I found my dog unconscious and I can't wake him — do something."

The vet lays the dog on the examination table and after a few simple tests he says, "I'm sorry, I don't feel a pulse, I'm afraid your dog is dead".

The lady can't accept this and says, "No, no, he can't be dead — do something else."

The vet goes into the other room, and comes back with a little cat. The cat jumps up on the table and starts sniffing the dog from head to toe. It sniffs and sniffs up and down the dog, then all of a sudden just stops and jumps off the table and leaves. "Well, that confirms it," the vet says, "your dog is dead."

The lady is very upset but finally settles down. "Okay, I guess you're right. How much do I owe you?" The vet says, "That will be $340."

The lady has a fit and asks, "Why is it so much? After all the vet didn't do anything for the dog."

"Well", the vet replied, "it's $40 for the office visit and $300 for the CAT SCAN!"

Note

CAT SCAN

CAT (or CT) scan is a method of examining body organs by scanning them with X rays and using a computer to construct a series of images. It is usually quite expensive.

Apparently the joke has a satirical tone in talking about a sniffing cat that makes the lady pay $300. The cat in the joke surely cannot bring the dead dog back to life. As it is spelt the same as CAT used for medical purposes, it *alludes* (暗指) to the unnecessary medical examinations done by doctors on the patients.

Unit 16

Talking About the Future

Preview

This unit integrates various useful expressions and authentic talks about the future.

Objectives

After studying this unit, the students are expected to:
1. know the basic words and expressions that are used to talk about the future;
2. understand conversations and short talks about what may happen in the future;
3. be able to talk about the future with other people.

Part A Language Focus

Notes

1. **futurologist, futurist**

   A futurologist is a person who is an expert in futurology, i.e. the study of how people live in the future. A futurist is one who studies and predicts the future especially on the basis of current trends.

2. **predict, foretell, forecast, foresee**

   These four words are more or less similar in meaning. The word "predict" is a very general word used to say that something will happen in the future. People use "foretell" to tell what will happen in the future, sometimes by using special magical powers. The word "forecast" is used when a statement is made about what is likely to happen in the future, based on the information that people have now. When people think or know that something is going to happen in the future, the word "foresee" is used.

3. **anticipate, expect**

The word "anticipate" means "to expect that something will happen and be ready for it". The word "expect" means "to believe with confidence, or think it likely, that an event will happen in the future". Depending on the context, "expect" may also mean "wait for anticipated thing."

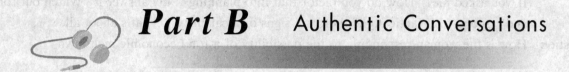

Part B   Authentic Conversations

Purpose

This part aims to familiarize the students with authentic conversations that can be heard in our daily life when people talk about the future.

Detailed Plan

1. Study the new words and expressions in *Word Bank*.
2. Do the required exercises.
3. Check the answers.
4. Listen to the conversations again. Pay special attention to the parts you didn't understand or misunderstood. You may refer to the script if necessary.

Short Conversations

Listening Script

Directions: You will hear 6 conversations between two speakers. Listen to them and answer the following questions by choosing the right options.

1. Man: Ten years from now, what will the Internet look like? Can you tell us what you think the Internet will look like?

   Woman: Well, what I hope it looks like is it's a place that you can securely do all sorts of online transactions. I think that's something that people are really worried about today.

   Question: What is the people's concern about the Internet today?

2. **Woman**: What do you think the entertainment industry will look like 20 years from today?

Man: The desire to hear a well-told story will never leave us, but the way in which stories are created and delivered will change immensely in the next 20 years. These changes, although birthed in culture, are ultimately driven by technology.

Question: What will most obviously change the entertainment industry in the next 20 years?

3. **Man**: Reading the headlines, there's a lot to worry about: rising oil prices, growing trade and budget deficits, pension plans failing, and so on. How worried are you about the chances of a total economic meltdown?

Woman: If you asked me for odds, I would say there's a 5% to 10% chance of real severe distress. If you asked me, "How do you factor that into planning?" my answer is "Watch out for it and respond to it tactically if there are signs of a calamity." That's about all.

Question: How is the woman responding to the possibility of a total economic meltdown?

4. **Woman**: In future, will global companies retain their national identities? Will IBM continue to be known as an American company, Siemens a German one?

Man: Oh, that will continue. They may be global, and the world may claim them, but we all know where they're from. That's part of the interplay between the dynamics of a cultural change and the dynamics of economic change.

Question: What will happen to global companies in future?

5. **Man**: You published four books with "mega" in the title. You could be said to own the word. Why not extend the franchise with your new book?

Woman: The short answer is I thought it was wearing a little thin and I needed a fresh kind of presentation.

Question: Why doesn't the woman use "mega" in the title of her new book?

6. **Woman**: Today women are better educated, more financially powerful, have improved health care and continue to outlive men. How do you think these female baby boomers will change our current definition of retirement?

Man: Well, I think, there's going to be a big lack of people to fill skilled service jobs in the next 10 or 15 years. And I hope these baby boomer women don't retire, continue to work and take advantage of those extra six or seven years that they live longer than the other gender.

Question: How much longer do women live than men according to the conversation?

Key

1. B   2. A   3. B   4. A   5. D   6. B

Notes

1. online transactions

An online transaction refers to any transaction involving money taking place via the Internet. There are different types of online transactions.

e.g. banking online, buying and selling online, paying bills online and so on.

2. **Siemens**

Siemens is a leading German manufacturer and supplier in all commercial electronics industries worldwide. They have several International manufacturing and operations locations.

3. **mega**

"Mega" can be used as a prefix, meaning "very large or great". It is sometimes used together with other words as attractive book titles.

4. **was wearing a little thin**

If something is wearing thin, you are bored with it because it is not interesting any more, or has become annoying.

e.g. *That joke has been told so many times and it's beginning to wear thin.*

5. **baby boomers**

Baby boomers are people who were born between 1946 and 1964. After American soldiers returned home from World War II in 1946, the United States experienced an explosion of births that continued for the next 18 years, when the birth rate began to drop.

Longer Conversations

Conversation One

Listening Script

Directions: You will hear a conversation between two speakers. Listen to the conversation twice and answer the questions by choosing the right options.

Woman: Do you have a prediction that's ripe for coming true soon?

Man: Well, I have one that's just come true. I wrote in the 1980's in my first book, that blind people will be able to take tiny device weighing a few ounces out of their pocket and read all the printed words that we see around us, and we did, a couple of months ago, introduce this reading machine in a four-ounce cell phone that can read in seven languages and translate one language to another.

Woman: You did?

Man: Yes. You can open up the cell phone and it will translate — it will read and translate into seven languages. There's about 1,000 guys and gals going around now reading signs on the wall, bank ATM displays, menus, handouts at meetings with this cell phone, which is — which works as a cell phone or a web browser. There's also a GPS system, all with voice output for the blind or dyslexic.

Woman: Wow, and how soon can I get one of these or anybody? Or are you keeping to yourself, to those thousand people?

Man: No, this is a product. People can go to our website and all the information on how to buy one is on it.

Questions:

1. What did the man predict in his first book in the 1980's?
2. How many languages can the reading machine read and translate?
3. Where is the reading system installed?
4. How can people get information about the product?

Key

1. B   2. C   3. A   4. B

Notes

1. **ounce**

   It is a unit for measuring weight, equal to 28.35 grams.

2. **ATM**

   ATM stands for "automated teller machine". It is an electronic machine that enables customers to withdraw paper money or carry out other banking transactions.

3. **dyslexic**

   The dyslexic are those who have a developmental disability in reading or spelling. To a dyslexic, letters and words may appear reversed. For example, *d* seen as *b* or *was* seen as *saw*. Many dyslexics never learn to read or write effectively, although they tend to show above average intelligence in other areas.

Conversation Two

Listening Script

Directions: You will hear a conversation between two speakers. Listen to the conversation twice and answer the questions by choosing the right options.

Man: Twenty years ago CBS did a five part series predicting what things would be like in 15 years in 2001. Now it's 2006 and we are curious about how good their predictions were.

Woman: They predict by 2001 the Russians could land on Mars.

Man: It would be funny if the Martians got to earth first, wouldn't it?

Woman: Los Angeles will be the nation's largest metropolis in 2001.

Man: Wrong, New York is still the largest.

Woman: The fastest growing, Phoenix.

Man: Wrong again, the fastest growing cities are Los Angeles and Las Vegas. I'd like to move to the slowest growing city.

Woman: So what we now call the bathroom will take on a whole new meaning. With whirlpool, saunas and exercise equipment it becomes an entertainment center.

Man: We still call it the bathroom. Never hear anyone at CBS say "Pardon me, I have to go to the entertainment center."

Woman: By 2001, Mexico City could well be the world's largest with perhaps 35 million.

Man: Wrong, it's 2006 and Mexico City is still only 20 million.

Woman: Prediction, Americans will work just six hours a day, just 30 hours a week.

Man: Wrong, I don't know anyone who works as little as six hours a day.

Woman: CBS News doesn't predict the future anymore. It's hard enough for them to tell us what happened today. Forget about tomorrow.

Questions:

1. Which of the following predictions was not made by CBS?
2. How many people are there in Mexico City in 2006?
3. What conclusion does the woman make about the predictions done by CBS?

Key

1. D 2. A 3. B

Notes

1. **Phoenix**

   Phoenix is the capital and largest city in the US state of Arizona. It is a center for agricultural products and information technology.

2. **Mexico City**

   It is the capital city of Mexico, built on the ruins of an ancient *Aztec*（阿兹特克人的）city.

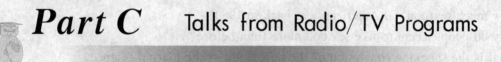

Part C   Talks from Radio/TV Programs

Purpose

This part consists of exercises based on talks excerpted from Radio/TV programs. The students are expected to understand such talks and get the necessary information from them.

Detailed Plan

1. Study the new words and expressions in *Word Bank*.
2. Do the exercises based on *Excerpt One* and *Excerpt Two*.
3. Check the answers.
4. Listen to the short talks again. Pay special attention to the parts you didn't understand or misunderstood. You may refer to the script if necessary.

Excerpt One

Listening Script

Directions: You will hear a short talk from a radio program. Listen to it twice and answer the questions by choosing the right options.

We are a nation that likes our seafood: sushi, salmon, crab cakes, and cod. In the US we eat an average of 16 and a half pounds of seafood per person each year, and that's half again as much as we ate back in 1960. And part of the reason we like our fish is the growing evidence that fish is good for us. A recent study from the Institute of Medicine concluded that fish is good for the heart and recommends that we keep seafood in our diet. So all that's the good news, now for the bad news.

By mid-century there may not be enough seafood to go around. A new study out in last week's issue of the journal *Science* reaches a really shocking conclusion that by the year 2048 there may be little sustainable fish or seafood left in the oceans. Over-fishing is partly to blame, the researchers say, but the bigger problem is that our management — or you might call it our mismanagement — of the oceans has left them over-fished, polluted, and without protection for fish habitats. That has led to a loss of biodiversity in the ocean that goes hand in hand with steeply declining fish numbers.

But the study holds out some hope for the seafood lover in you. Remember, there is time to change the projected outcome if we change the way we manage our oceans.

Questions:

1. How much seafood did Americans eat back in 1960?
2. Why do people seem to like seafood more than before?
3. What is the shocking conclusion of the new study in the journal Science?
4. What shall we do in order to have a steady supply of seafood in the future?

Key

1. B 2. B 3. B 4. D

Notes

1. **sushi**

   Sushi is a traditional Japanese food made with rice and other ingredients, often including fish.

2. **the Institute of Medicine**

   The Institute of Medicine is a not-for-profit, non-governmental American organization established in 1970 under the charter of the National Academy of Sciences. It provides independent, objective, evidence-based advice to policymakers, health professionals, the private sector, and the public.

3. **the journal *Science***

   Science is the academic journal of the American Association for the Advancement of Science and is considered one of the world's most prestigious scientific journals. The major focus of the journal is publishing important original scientific research and research reviews.

Excerpt Two

Listening Script

Directions: You will hear a short talk from a TV program. Listen to it twice and answer the questions by choosing the right options.

Fareed Zakaria: What is the Internet going to look like 10 years from now?

Bill Gates: Well, the thing that I think people are underestimating is that the shape of the computers that are connected up will be very different. You know, a tablet-type reading device, ability to walk in the room and it can see who's coming in. You can just talk. Your walls — screens will be very cheap, so your walls will — you'll be able to have sort of virtual wallpaper, anything that you're interested in. You know, you hear your parents walking down the hall, you change it to something else. Or you have your grandmother visiting, you change it to what she might be interested in.

Zakaria: Is some of the innovation coming from outside the United States now in a way that it wasn't 10 or 15 years ago?

Gates: Absolutely. The computer market 15 years ago, you could say the most demanding customers were in the United States. And so, if you could satisfy their needs, you just basically took the same thing and sold it worldwide. You did some localization.

Today, the penetration of cell phones is actually higher in other countries. China's got more broadband users than any country in the world. And India really goes fast, that'll be the case for the rest of the century.

So, you have to be far more global in terms of seeing what customers are doing, and having bright people who work on those problems. And so, all the technology companies are figuring out how we gather that customer input on a broader basis than ever before, how we work with more universities on their research programs than ever before. And I'm very proud of the way that Microsoft has done that. It's one of the things that has driven our success.

Zakaria: Do you think history will remember you as the man who created Microsoft, or the man who created the Gates Foundation?

Gates: You know, who knows how history will think of me? You know, the person who played bridge with Warren Buffett, maybe. Or maybe not at all.

Questions:

1. What does Bill Gates think of people's attitude towards the development of the Internet?

2. What kind of walls will people have at home in the future according to Gill Gates?

3. What was Microsoft's research strategy 15 years ago?

4. What are the two things that Microsoft is doing to guarantee its success?

5. How will history think of Bill Gates according to Gates' own opinion?

Key

1. C 2. A 3. A 4. D 5. D

Notes

1. **Fareed Zakaria**

   Fareed Zakaria（1964— ）is an India-born American journalist, author, and television host. He also hosts an international affairs program, *Fareed Zakaria GPS*, which airs Sundays worldwide on CNN.

2. **Bill Gates**

   Born in 1955, Bill Gates cofounded Microsoft in 1975 and as chairman built it into one of the largest computer software manufacturers in the world.

3. **the Gates Foundation**

   This refers to the Bill & Melinda Gates Foundation, which is annotated in Unit 12.

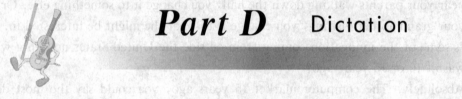

Part D   Dictation

Purpose

This part contains a short talk to be dictated to the students. This exercise trains the students' skills in writing down what they have heard.

Detailed Plan

1. Study the new words and expressions in *Word Bank*.
2. Listen to the short talk from the beginning to the end without any pause.
3. Write down the sentences during the pauses when the short talk is spoken again.
4. Read the listening script and correct whatever mistakes the students may have made.
5. Listen to the short talk again if necessary.

Listening Script

Directions: Listen to a short talk twice. When you listen to it the first time, you should listen carefully for its general idea. When you listen to it the second time, you are required to fill in the blanks numbered from 1 to 8 with the exact words you have just heard. For blanks numbered from 9 to 11 you are required to fill the missing information with the exact words you have just heard or write down the main points in your own words.

Albert Einstein remarked in 1932 that "there is not the slightest indication that nuclear energy will ever be <u>obtainable</u>." Thomas Edison thought alternating <u>current</u> would be a waste of time. Franklin Delano Roosevelt once predicted, when he was Assistant <u>Secretary</u> of the Navy, that airplanes would never be useful in battle against a <u>fleet</u> of ships. There's nothing like the passage of time to make the world's smartest people look like complete <u>idiots</u>.

Why is <u>predicting</u> the future so difficult? After all, if history is just one thing after another, <u>shouldn't</u> the future be more of the same? But over and over again, even our most highly educated guesses go <u>disastrously</u> wrong.

Of course, <u>the smart play would be not to try to guess what's coming next</u>. But trapped as we are in the one-way flow of time, not predicting the future would be like driving a car without bothering to glance through the windshield from time to time. We desperately need prophets, even false ones, <u>to help us get a glimpse of the future that lies ahead of us</u>.

We humans are gamblers by nature, but we're not stupid gamblers: <u>we need to know what the odds are and what we should do accordingly</u>.

Key

1. obtainable
2. current
3. Secretary
4. fleet
5. idiots
6. predicting
7. shouldn't
8. disastrously
9. the smart play would be not to try to guess what's coming next
10. to help us get a glimpse of the future that lies ahead of us
11. we need to know what the odds are and what we should do accordingly

Notes

1. Thomas Edison

Thomas Edison (1847—1931) was one of the world's greatest inventors. He received a record of 1,093 patents for devices he invented on his own or with others. His best-known inventions include the *phonograph* (留声机), the light bulb, and the motion-picture projector. Edison also created the first power station in the United States, in 1882.

2. Franklin Delano Roosevelt

Franklin Delano Roosevelt (1882—1945) was the only US president elected to the office four times. He led the United States through two of the greatest crises of the 20th century: the Great Depression (1929—1939) and World War II (1939—1945).

Part E   Fun Time

Listening Script

Directions: Listening to the song *Whatever Will Be*, *Will Be* sung by Doris Day. Learn to sing the song and fill in the missing words in the following lyrics.

Whatever Will Be, Will Be

When I was just a little girl
I asked my mother <u>what will I be</u>
Will I be pretty
<u>Will I be rich</u>
Here's what she said to me

Que sera sera
Whatever will be will be
The future's <u>not ours to see</u>
Que sera sera
What will be will be

When I <u>grew up</u> and fell in love
I asked my sweetheart what lies ahead
Will we have <u>rainbows</u> day after day
Here's what my sweetheart said

Que sera sera
Whatever will be will be
The future's not ours to see
Que sera sera

What will be, will be
Que sera sera . . .

Key

1. what will I be   2. Will I be rich   3. not ours to see   4. paint pictures   5. wise reply   6. grew up
7. rainbows

Note

Que Sera , Sera

　　Que Sera Sera (Whatever Will Be, Will Be), first published in 1956, is a popular song written by the Jay Livingston and Ray Evans songwriting team. The song was featured in Alfred Hitchcock's 1956 film, *The Man Who Knew Too Much*, with Doris Day and James Stewart in the lead roles. Day's recording of the song for Columbia Records was a hit in both the United States and the United Kingdom.

Test Yourself (Units 9~16)

Section A

Directions: In this section, you will hear 8 short conversations and 2 long conversations. At the end of each conversation, one or more questions will be asked about what was said. Both the conversation and the questions will be spoken only once. After each question there will be a pause. During the pause, you must read the four choices marked A, B, C and D, and decide which is the best answer.

1. Man: Is there anything that teenagers all seem to have in common as to why they are sleep-deprived?

   Woman: Well, lots of different things contribute to kids not getting enough sleep. We certainly know that teenagers' sleeping cycle does change a little bit as they get older, but we also know that there's a lot of competing demands on the time of teenagers.

   Question: Why are teenagers sleep-deprived according to the woman?

2. Woman: Does this surprise you, you know, as an educator that we know so little about these basic things about science?

   Man: It doesn't surprise me anymore because we've been living with this for some time. It's depressing. It's terribly depressing. It's alarming. It's dangerous, I think, for our future that so few people have a grasp of how science works and even less of a grasp for, you know, what's involved.

   Question: Why can't the man keep calm while talking about science?

3. Woman: How much of your personal belief system was shaped by religion and how much by your scientific career?

   Man: I grew up without religion. I'm in physics because I love physics. But I do hope that the advance of science, in general, and physics, in particular, will in the long run weaken the hold of religion on people's minds.

   Question: What is the man's attitude toward religion?

4. Man: Warren Buffet, who at the age of 75 has got a $44 billion fortune, said he plans to give about 85% of it to five charities. The lion's share will go to the Bill and Melinda Gates Foundation. This is by far the largest charitable gift ever.

   Woman: My mom always says it's always good to give, you know? And say you'll be blessed for that.

   Question: What is the woman's reaction to Buffet's donation?

5. Woman: You run Independent News & Media, which has interests in newspapers in Ireland,

England, India and Africa. Isn't print dead?

Man: In a time-starved world, a brilliant newspaper is a very cheap way to make money. If it's well put together, you can, in half an hour, get from that what you would spend six hours from the Internet doing. The newspaper industry is growing, quite slowly, but it is growing.

Question: What does the man think of the newspaper industry?

6. Woman: You don't look happy these days. What's bothering you?

Man: I'm going to lose my job if our sales figures keep going down. I cannot control the situation because I don't own the company. Things are going to be tough until the world economy gets better.

Question: What is the man worried about?

7. Woman: Now the Tuesday earthquake off the coast of Northern California was an undersea quake. That was supposed to trigger a tsunami warning, but nothing happened, did it?

Man: Well, that's right. In this type of earthquakes, the ground moves sideways rather than up and down. So huge masses of water aren't lifted or dropped, which is what's necessary to create a tsunami.

Question: Why didn't the Tuesday earthquake trigger a tsunami?

8. Man: Do you know what to do during a lightning storm — how to protect yourself, what to teach your children?

Woman: I generally get in a closed truck or a car when I am outside, because lightning will travel around, but not through the metal body of a vehicle. I don't let my children talk on the phone during a storm or use home appliances. Lightning can pass through electrical wiring.

Question: What shouldn't children do during a lightning storm according to the woman?

Long Conversation 1

Woman: What one word would you use to describe this whole crazy ride of yours?

Man: Compelling. I — I've had a — a joyous ride for 50 years. It's what I always wanted to do, what I dreamed of doing. When I was five years old, I'd look up at the radio and imitate the radio announcers. I'd pretend that it was my show. I would go and — honest to god — in my bathroom go:

"This is the CBS Radio Network. And now a tale well calculated to keep you in suspense." So ...

Woman: When you were just five?

Man: Five, six. I'd imitate anything I heard. I'd go to ball games and broadcast the game to myself.

So I'm living out a dream. In fact, the last time I worked was 50 years ago for the United Parcel Service. I was a helper on the truck. I was a delivery boy. And then I went down to Miami and broke in. So I — compelling fits it.

Woman: Why do you think, Larry, in a business that can be pretty tough, you have endured for so

Man: Oh, that's hard to self-examine. It's a good question. I don't know. First, I've had supportive management, pretty much all the way, from the first people that hired me who liked me, to the Ted Turners, to the current group at CNN, to the people in radio all those years. So they were — they let me — they let me be me, which is the key in this business. And I think I've always been me. And I think that comes through to people.

Questions 9 to 11 are based on the conversation you have just heard.
9. What kind of dream did Larry King have when he was young?
10. How did Larry King earn his living 50 years ago?
11. What contributed to Larry King's success as a TV host?

Long Conversation 2
Neil Cavuto, Host: Well, imagine never having to worry about hurricanes and energy impact. Imagine never having to gas up your car again or recharge your cell phone, an endless supply of energy that does not harm the environment and won't cost you a dime. In fact, it comes from thin air. My next guest says the technology exists. Here to explain how it works is Sean McCarthy. He's CEO of a company called Steorn. It's a technology firm based in Ireland. Good to have you, sir.

Sean McCarthy, CEO, Steorn Ltd.: Good evening.
Cavuto: This almost sounds too good to be true. Now, I know you're a genius, but if you could explain it in layman's terms for me.
McCarthy: What — what we've done is, about three years ago, we developed a way of constructing magnetic fields, so that, when you travel around the fields, you suffer a net gain of energy. This energy, we have proven over the years, doesn't come from any other source. What that means, in terms of a product, is — is, quite literally, that, you know, if we deploy this as — as a replacement for your car engine, you will never have to put gas into your car. We — we replace the battery in your cell phone; you will never have to recharge your phone.
Cavuto: But where is the energy coming from, Sean?
McCarthy: Literally, there has never been an identifiable source for the energy. What this technology is doing is — is directly contradicting one of the basic laws of physics, the principle of the conservation of energy. So, what we did last week is to issue a challenge to the world of science, to ask them to come and to test it, and to let the public know that this kind of technology exists.
Cavuto: So, and they — they were impressed by what they saw, something about the magnet images or — or presence that — that — that makes this work. My immediate reaction to that was, is there any hazard, danger, cancer-causing type vulnerability here, anything like that?
McCarthy: No. I mean, anything that has electrical energy in it generates a magnetic field. The kind of magnetic fields we're looking at here are very low-level. And the technology itself is — is shielded. So, there is no discernible magnetic field, outside of the technology itself.

Questions 12 to 15 are based on the conversation you have just heard.

12. What does the TV host think of the new technology?

13. How does the new technology work in principle?

14. What is unusual about this technology?

15. What is the TV host worried about as far as the technology is concerned?

Key

1. D 2. C 3. C 4. D 5. B 6. B 7. C 8. C 9. C 10. A 11. A 12. D 13. B 14. A 15. C

Section B

Directions: In this section, you will hear 3 short passages. At the end of each passage, you will hear some questions. Both the passage and the questions will be spoken only once. After you hear a question, you must choose the best answer from the four choices marked A, B, C and D.

Passage One

When I was growing up I remember my mother saying dozens of times, "Live your life so that at the end of it you'll have no regrets." She sure did. She was her city's first female pilot, took a six-month bicycling tour of Europe in 1936, raised three girls and helped my dad build their retirement house. She did all the things she wanted to do and died at peace with her life in 2001 at age 88.

Living my life so I'd have no regrets was a lesson I took in and believed in, too. I saved dimes and quarters while paying my way through college to fund my own three-month European trip. I've gone up in a hot-air balloon, traveled extensively, worked for good causes in my church and taught hundreds of children to read during my 23-plus-year career as a special education teacher in Massachusetts public schools. My husband Dave and I raised three happy, productive children and enjoy our eight grandchildren.

A year ago, unexpectedly, I was diagnosed with lung cancer. Since then, I've had surgeries and several rounds of chemotherapy. Statistics say I have about another year to live. Maybe I do and maybe I'll have more time. No matter. I refuse to let cancer change my philosophy. When I feel well, I pack in as many experiences as I can. I visit friends, travel, laugh, read wonderful novels, play with our grandchildren and cherish those I love. I believe in living my life. At some point, hopefully much later than the doctors predict, I'll feel too sick to enjoy what used to give me pleasure. Then, I hope to do just as my mother did. I'll say to anyone who'll listen, "I believe you should live your life so that at the end of it you will have no regrets."

Questions 16 to 18 are based on the passage you have just heard.

16. What did the speaker's mother do in 1936?

17. What activity does the speaker love as much as her mother?

18. What has given the speaker her courage and strength to enjoy her life in spite of her illness?

Passage Two

If you feel the earth shaking under your feet, get under something heavy to avoid being hit by falling objects. If indoors, take shelter under a sturdy table or other heavy furniture object. Standing under a door frame can offer protection as it is usually the strongest part of a building. An inside corner of the house can also offer protection. Do not run outdoors as you may be hit by falling debris. Stay away from glass objects, mirrors, and windows.

If you are outside, stay there. If on a hill, watch for rock slides — getting to the top is safest. Keep away from tall buildings, trees, power lines, and any other collapsible object. Cover your head as much as possible. If the earthquake is strong enough to cause you to lose your balance, lie flat on the ground. Stay out of basements, subways, or tunnels, which could become blocked.

If you're in a car, stop and stay put. Dive for the floor and crouch below the seat level if possible.

When the earthquake has stopped, watch out for fallen cables, broken roads, and damaged buildings and bridges that could collapse.

If your house seems okay, enter carefully (if outside during the quake) and check for fire, gas leaks, and water leaks. Don't smoke or light a match. Use only a flashlight. Turn off gas, water, and electricity if you suspect any hazard or are advised to do so by local authorities.

If your house is damaged, consider building a shelter from available debris. Some experts feel it's safer to stay in a temporary shelter than to return to a damaged building.

Questions 19 to 21 are based on the passage you have just heard.

19. What are you suggested to do in the house when an earthquake takes place?
20. What are you suggested to do when an earthquake has stopped?
21. What does the passage mainly talk about?

Passage Three

When I get on a plane to fly from Haines to Juneau, there's always a safety talk. This includes the usual seat belt, life preserver and emergency exit instructions. Often, the pilot makes a little joke about no running up and down the aisles. This gets a chuckle because the plane is too small to even stand up in. Then he, or sometimes she, says, "There's a fire extinguisher underneath my seat and an emergency bucket in the back". I find it extremely reassuring.

The first thing I do every time I get in a small plane is pray that it makes it safely to the airport. This is not an idle prayer. Two different pilots have owned the house next door to me. Both are dead, killed in plane crashes. I know more people who have died in planes than in cars. And that influences my response to flying more than all the statistics about risk.

Soon, I'm getting on another plane. My family is traveling to New York for Thanksgiving because that's where people I love are. Now more than ever, I want to be near them. When we get on the transcontinental flight in Seattle, I hope the stewardess tells us what to do if the plane gets hijacked. I hope she lets us know exactly what new security measures are in place, both on the plane and in the airport. That, along with the glass of wine, should help me stay calm.

Questions 22 to 25 are based on the passage you have just heard.

22. What does the author think of the pilot's safety talk when he flies from Haines to Juneau?
23. Why does the author chuckle when the pilot makes a little joke about no running up and down the aisles?
24. What will the author do whenever he gets on a plane?

25. What does the author expect most from the stewardess when he and his family get on the transcontinental flight?

Key

16. C 17. C 18. D 19. A 20. B 21. A 22. D 23. A 24. B 25. A

Section C

Directions: In this section, you will hear a passage three times. When the passage is read for the first time, you should listen carefully for its general idea. When the passage is read for the second time, you are required to fill in the blanks numbered from 26 to 33 with the exact words you have just heard. For blanks numbered from 34 to 36 you are required to fill in the missing information. For these blanks, you can either use the exact words you have just heard or write down the main points in your own words. Finally, when the passage is read for the third time, you should check what you have written.

Omen is a sign of future good or bad luck. A good omen <u>foretells</u> a desirable event, and a bad omen <u>forecasts</u> disaster. For example, a person may <u>regard</u> a dream about gold as an omen of success in business. Or the person may believe that the death of a <u>relative</u> will follow a dream about losing a tooth. Sometimes omens come from a deliberate <u>attempt</u> to look into the future, such as a <u>fortuneteller's</u> tarot cards.

Many ancient societies believed that <u>lightning</u>, thunder, or the behavior of animals foretold events. For example, the Mesopotamians thought fire would <u>destroy</u> the king's palace if a dog were seen lying on the throne. In Greece, <u>the cry of a hawk warned of danger</u>. Many leaders, when trying to decide on a course of action, asked the gods for a sign. In folklore, many heroes die after ignoring such signs.

<u>Omens may be considered either good or bad depending on their interpretation</u>. The same sign may be interpreted differently by different people or different cultures. For example, in Western history, black cats have often been looked upon as a symbol of evil omens; <u>in other cultures they are considered to be good omens</u>.

Key

26. foretells 27. forecasts 28. regard 29. relative 30. attempt 31. fortuneteller's 32. lightning
33. destroy
34. the cry of a hawk warned of danger
35. Omens may be considered either good or bad depending on their interpretation
36. in other cultures they are considered to be good omens

郑 重 声 明

　　高等教育出版社依法对本书享有专有出版权。任何未经许可的复制、销售行为均违反《中华人民共和国著作权法》，其行为人将承担相应的民事责任和行政责任，构成犯罪的，将被依法追究刑事责任。为了维护市场秩序，保护读者的合法权益，避免读者误用盗版书造成不良后果，我社将配合行政执法部门和司法机关对违法犯罪的单位和个人给予严厉打击。社会各界人士如发现上述侵权行为，希望及时举报，本社将奖励举报有功人员。

反盗版举报电话：(010)58581897/58581896/58581879

传　　真：(010)82086060

E-mail：dd@hep.com.cn

通信地址：北京市西城区德外大街 4 号
　　　　　　高等教育出版社打击盗版办公室

邮　　编：100120

购书请拨打电话：(010)58581118